IN TOO DEEP

BY: SHERRY D. FICKLIN

For Lisa C.
Warrior, Poet, Friend

In Too Deep
Copyright ©2016 Sherry D. Ficklin
All rights reserved.

ISBN:978-1-63422-163-4
Cover Design by: Marya Heiman
Typography by: Courtney Nuckels
Editing by: Cynthia Shepp

For more information about our content disclosure, please utilize the QR code above with your smart phone or visit us at

www.CleanTeenPublishing.com.

ONE

"YOU DON'T HAVE TO DO THIS, YOU KNOW," I OFFER halfheartedly, knowing deep down that if he were to walk away right now, I'd go with him.

The wind blows a chunk of chestnut hair into my eyes and I brush it away, tucking it behind my ear. Below us, the waves crash into the legs of the pier like a beating pulse, slow and steady. I take a deep breath, centering myself. Beside me, Cole chuckles as he slips off his leather jacket, draping it across the railing.

"What, you think I'd rather be at the Spring Formal?"

The side of my mouth turns up in a grin before I can stop it. The idea of spending the night surrounded by taffeta-covered pom-squaders makes me want to stab myself in the leg with a spork—a feeling I know Cole shares. Of course, he'd at least been asked to the dance. I, however, remain painfully solo. Not that I'd have gone either way, but being asked would have been nice.

"Besides," he continues, reaching out to take my hand. "I promised Ollie I'd look out for you, Farris."

My grin falters as the last bits of red-purple daylight fade to gray, as if the color is being drained from the world. My boyfriend Oliver and his family were re-stationed to NAS Whidbey Island three months ago. At first, we video chatted every day. Then it became weekly emails. Now all I get is the occasional text message. I'm not bitter about it. It's not like I hadn't expected it, after all. It's just what happens when people move away—something I know all too well as a military brat. Still, some small, lonely place in my heart aches. Now, we are stuck in that odd, uncomfortable place between being together and being apart, not entirely sure where we stand.

Cole, one of Oliver's best friends, promised to look after me in Ollie's absence, and he's been as good as his word. He showed up at my door while I was cramming for the SATs with a bag of Moo Shu Pork in one hand and a six-pack of Mountain Dew in the other. When I was sick, he brought me soup and boxes of tissues. I can't even count the number of nights we spent talking or shooting pool, all the times he helped me keep putting one foot in front of the other when all I wanted to do was let myself sit stagnant.

Basically, there are friends who help you move, and there are friends who help you move *bodies*.

Cole is the latter.

But tonight, well, tonight is something else entirely. I shiver, the waves crashing below me churning like a blender. My hands clench, my jaw aching from holding my chattering teeth together. Inside my chest, my heart stutters painfully.

Tonight is the anniversary of my mother's death. I'd been prepared to come here alone, to face my fears alone.

I should have known that wasn't going to happen. My eyes slide to the right, to the boy standing at my side.

Beside me, Cole is quiet, his free hand casually stuffed in his jean pocket, like he isn't standing fifty feet over the crashing ocean, perched on the edge of a railing along the pier. He isn't looking at me, but his square chin is turned up, his gaze on the stars just becoming visible in the sky. He's waiting for me to say something, or that's what it feels like, but there are no words for what's churning inside me now. Just a wash of grief and fear, mixed with a deep gratitude, all jumbled up inside.

Mom is buried back in her hometown of Charleston, so I can't even go visit her grave. Dad's off in Turkey doing training exercises with his squadron, which leaves me here, alone. Well, I glance over at Cole. Not quite alone.

I squeeze his hand, and he looks down at me.

"You scared, Farris?" he asks, a hint of challenge

in his voice.

I frown, fighting back my near panic. "Not really."

He raises an eyebrow. "Oh?"

"Terrified is more accurate," I admit. "But that's the point, right?"

"Hey, it's your party; I'm just here for the cupcakes."

I should chuckle, but I don't. Instead, I look down at my dark blue Converse and the black water below. The tide is high—I'd been careful to make sure of that. I'd done the math carefully, making sure there were no unnecessary risks tonight. I'm not looking to kill myself, after all. Just to push myself. To conquer the fear I've been holding onto for far too long. My mother always said it was only in overcoming our fears that we could find our true selves. I really hope she was right because at this moment, I feel like I have no idea who I am anymore. It isn't just missing Ollie and Mom that's taking its toll on me; it's looking down the road at college and being on my own—really on my own—for the first time.

It's enough to make any girl want to jump off a bridge.

For as long as I can remember, I've had this nightmare where I'm drowning. I don't think it's ever going to go away, but maybe, just maybe, this will help. Freud says drowning in dreams is an internal struggle against yourself—a need to break free or come clean.

I fit into all those categories.

All this psychosis in a fun, candy shell.

Pushing back the thoughts, I clear my mind, focusing on the feel of Cole's hand in mine, on the small, steady beat of his pulse that I can feel in his fingers. I let it calm me, focusing on it until everything else feels distant.

"On the count of three?" I ask.

Cole nods. "One," he says. "Two."

In unison, we bend our knees and yell, "Three!"

We leap, the cold sea air cradling us for only a heartbeat before plunging us into the swirling darkness below.

I RELEASE HIS HAND A MOMENT BEFORE WE HIT THE water, the icy cold waves like shattered glass as I drive through the surface feet-first. Every inch of my skin stings on impact, the oxygen pushed from my lungs. Below the surface, I feel a wave roll over me, the tide dragging me toward the shore.

Kicking my legs, I finally surface, sucking in a deep breath just before another wave crashes over me, threatening to take me back under. It's only luck that allows me to bob above the water, wiping the hair back from my face. I open my eyes. A few feet away, I see Cole break the surface, gasping for air. Whipping around, he searches for me in the darkness. Catching sight of me, he laughs, cupping his hand and dragging it across the water, sending a spray at my face.

I splash him back, feeling giddy as the adrenaline floods my system. It's a dizzy, relieved high, sort of like the feeling you get at the end of a roller coaster ride. Part of me is just glad to be alive, the other much braver part cheers to do it again. Just then, a familiar tug grabs me as the tide begins to pull me back out to sea. With a jerk of my head, I turn and swim for shore, checking to make sure Cole is following.

As soon as I feel the sand under my feet, I stand up and begin walking to the shore. Within minutes, Cole is beside me, wringing the water out of his black T-shirt.

Every step is labored, the waves pushing and pulling against my legs. My denim shorts and pale green tank top are soaked and heavy. Even the wind blowing across my bare arms hurts as we hike onto the shore and collapse to our knees, laughing.

I roll onto my back, too elated to care about the sand sticking all over me. The moon is just rising on the horizon, huge and full, its light bouncing off the choppy surface of the water.

"Feel better?" Cole asks, still catching his breath.

I put my hands on my chest. "Yeah, I kinda do."

We sit there like that for a few minutes, just enjoying the rush of adrenaline and the sound of the waves fracturing against the sand. Finally, he breaks the silence.

"What's that?" he asks, jerking his head down the beach.

I roll over, squinting against the darkness. A huge lump of something has rolled up on shore a few yards down from us. My first thought is that it looks like a black trash bag. Then I see something else, something that looks a lot like a hand.

"I think that's a person," I say, climbing to my feet.

Cole is already upright, jogging toward them. As soon as he gets there, he stops, dropping to his knees and reaching out. I follow behind. The closer I get, the more the crumpled body comes into focus. Cole rolls him onto his back and puts two fingers on his neck, checking for a pulse.

There's no point, really. His face is waxen and swollen, his eyes wide and milky white, staring up at nothingness. His blue lips are parted, white sea foam bubbling from his mouth. The face is familiar; it's a boy from our school. Not someone I know well, but someone I've seen around enough to recognize.

"That's Mac," I say.

Cole clasps his palms against Mac's chest and starts doing compressions, but I put a hand on his shoulder, stopping him. It's too late. Much too late.

Mac is dead.

As I stare at him, time slows down around me.

Suddenly, I can see every tiny detail of him. The tiny scar under his chin, the red welts on the side of his neck. He's in a tuxedo, like he'd been at the dance, but his socks and shoes are missing. There's a cuff link missing from his right sleeve, I notice, taking mental inventory. Probably all lost in the tide.

"Where's your phone?" I hear myself asking.

"It's in my jacket, back on the dock."

I nod. "Go get it. Call 911."

Cole looks at me, then down at the body, and then back up at me. "I'm not leaving you here alone," he says, hesitating.

I shoot him an eye roll. Although to be perfectly honest, I feel the first twinges of real shock setting in as time snaps back into focus and I realize that my heart is beating fast—too fast—and I'm practically panting. "I'm fine. What's he going to do? Stare me to death?"

Cole adamantly shakes his head. "Come on," he demands, holding out his hand.

I take it reluctantly and let him tug me along as we jog back up to the boardwalk. As soon as we are out of the sand, he releases me and runs for the pier. I stand, hugging myself and watching from a distance as Mac's lifeless body lies in the sand, the water lapping up around his feet. I don't realize just how cold I've become until Cole returns, setting his jacket across my shoulders and rubbing my arms. I try to protest, some distant part of me is afraid of ruining his favorite jacket with my wet, sandy clothes, but the words refuse to come out. My throat is dry, my voice less than a whisper. As the sensation returns to my limbs, tiny slivers of pain erupt everywhere and I shake, my teeth chattering uncontrollably.

"Cops are on their way," he says, still trying to warm me.

I turn, burrowing my face into his wet chest, clutching him as I squeeze my eyes closed, trying in vain to fight off the image of Mac's dead eyes staring up at me. The shock is getting worse, but I fight to keep it at bay. Cole's arms snake around me, but it doesn't help. I don't move again until the sound of sirens cut through the still air. The next time I open my eyes, it's to see the red and blue lights dancing across Cole's worried face.

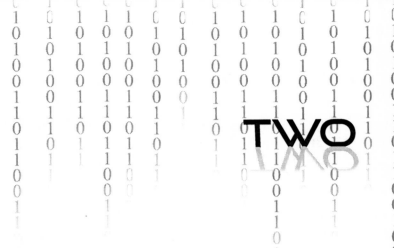

TWO

The police station is warm, thank God. Someone is kind enough to hand me a scratchy, brown blanket and shove a cup of coffee in my hand. They take Cole to a different area, but I can see him across the room, talking with one of the other detectives. He has a similar blanket wrapped around him, but no coffee. I try to give him a reassuring smile, but it feels more like a grimace.

"Why, exactly, were the three of you at the pier?"

I blink, looking back at the lady speaking. She's in black slacks and a hastily thrown on white blouse, buttoned up the front, with a dark gray blazer hanging on the back of her chair. Her red hair is cut short into a neat bob, the top held back with a black clip.

I frown. "No. I told you, it was just me and Cole. We skipped the dance to go to the pier together."

"So Nathan wasn't with you?"

I actually feel the look of irritation I'm giving her. We've been over this three times already. Nathan

'Mac' McKenzie wasn't a friend. He was barely an acquaintance.

"No. We didn't know anyone else was around at all until we came out of the water and saw him wash up on shore."

"Why were you swimming at all? It's a cold night, and you just thought it'd be fun to take a dip in your clothes?"

I take a sip of coffee before answering. It's old and bitter, but the warmth feels really nice as it fills my belly. "It was one of those impulsive things teenagers do." I lean forward, "Are you even allowed to be talking to me without a parent present?" I don't mention that I'm legally emancipated. No need to do her job for her.

Now it's her turn to frown. "You aren't a suspect, and we aren't questioning you. You called 911. We're just taking your statement."

I take another sip of coffee before answering. "So we can go then."

It's not a question.

She shoves a piece of paper at me and slaps a pen on top of it. "This is your formal statement, as you gave it to me. Please read over it, make sure it's accurate, and sign it."

I look over the document. It basically says exactly what I told her—that we found the body washed up on shore just after midnight. I quickly sign it. With a jerk toward Cole, I ask, "Can I get him a cup of coffee now? He's my ride home, and I'd rather not have his fingers too frozen to hold a steering wheel."

"I can have a patrol car take you home," she offers.

"Pass," I say, holding up a hand. That's just what I need, some nosy neighbor calling my dad to report that I've been brought home in a police car. "But thanks anyway."

She shrugs, nodding toward the corner of the room where the coffee machine sits. I walk over, fill a cup, and make a beeline for Cole, who is just signing his own paper.

When he stands, I hand him the cup. He pulls off his blanket and tosses it in his now-vacant chair.

"No, thank *you*, Detective Walters. It's been the highlight of my evening," he sternly says, putting his hand on my back to lead me out.

Once we're in his car, the heat cranked up as high as it will go, I finally allow myself to relax.

"Can you believe those people?" he complains, rubbing his hands together in front of the vent. "We call for help and they treat us like we are the criminals."

I shake my head. "I just can't believe they thought he was with us. I mean, he was in a tux, for shit's sake. He had obviously been at the dance."

"I'm just glad they didn't insist on calling your dad."

"I'm technically emancipated. He thought it was

best, just in case I needed anything while he was on detachment and I couldn't get a hold of him." I shrug. "You're lucky that you're already eighteen or they would have hauled your parents in for sure."

He chuckles. "I almost wish they had. If they thought dealing with me was bad, I would have loved to see them try to deal with my mother at three am."

I snicker at the thought. Cole's mom is all of four-foot-nine, maybe ninety pounds soaking wet, and one-hundred-percent spitfire. She doesn't deal with nonsense well and has zero tolerance for stupidity. I've seen her lose it on someone more than once, and I pity anyone on the other end of one of her tirades.

"What are you gonna tell her?" I ask.

"The truth," he says with a firm nod. "Tomorrow. But tonight, I'm going to let her get her eight hours of uninterrupted beauty rest."

"Solid plan."

"And you?" he slyly asks.

I frown. "Yeah. I pretty much need to email Dad ASAP. He has some kind of spidey sense about this kinda thing."

"And then?"

"And then I'm going to begin my new life of never closing my eyes or sleeping ever again. I don't think sweet dreams are going to be an option after this," I admit.

We pull up outside my house. Putting the car in

park, he pulls out the key.

"What are you doing?" I ask.

He rolls his eyes. "I'm couch surfing, obviously."

Shaking my head, I open the door and climb out. It won't be the first time Cole's crashed on the sofa, but it will be the first time he's done it on purpose. Last week, we'd both passed out during a *Star Wars* movie marathon. Somehow, this feels different.

"I don't need a babysitter," I say as I unlock the front door.

"And I don't need a lecture." He grins, brushing past me and heading for the living room. "Besides, it's not for you. It's for the rest of us. You get cranky when you don't sleep. It's a *for the good of mankind* thing really."

I snort, folding my arms across my chest as he flops onto the tan sofa. "And it has nothing at all to do with the fact that you don't want to go home?" I challenge.

He's been spending as much time as humanly possible away from his own house. His mom is dating a new guy Cole nicknamed Lieutenant Loser. Apparently, he makes Cole want to gouge his eyes out. I understand the feeling. My dad has only recently stepped back into the dating world. Just the thought of it makes my skin crawl. The difference is my mom is dead. His dad is still hoping for reconciliation, and though he'd never say it, I think Cole is too.

I walk to the hall cabinet and grab a thick, blue blanket and pillow, setting them on the couch. Cole flips on the flat screen and starts channel surfing. We aren't wet anymore, though my clothes are still cold and covered in salt and sand. A quick glance tells me his aren't any better. Going into Dad's room, I dig around until I find a plain white T-shirt and some green sweatpants.

"Here," I say, handing them to him over the back of the sofa. "Grab a shower and change into these. I'll toss your clothes in the wash."

He looks up from the TV and grins. In one smooth motion, he grabs the back of his shirt and pulls it over his head, balling it up and tossing it at my face. It smells like salt and seaweed, and under all that, it smells like something familiar, something spicy and sweet at the same time.

It smells like Cole.

"Can do," he says, crawling over the back of the couch and brushing past me, toward the bathroom.

I have to admit, the sight of Cole shirtless does not suck. He has a long torso and broad shoulders that accentuates every well-defined muscle. His jeans ride low on his hips, low enough to see the tan line from his board shorts. He catches me looking, and his grin widens.

"Watch out now, I'll tell everyone you were ogling my goodies."

I roll my eyes, fighting back a blush.

Once the door is closed and the water running, I tap gently before reaching inside and grabbing what's left of his clothes off the floor—closing the door behind me as I leave. When I get to the laundry room, I toss his clothes in the machine. Then, still listening to the sound of running water, I slip off my shirt and shorts and toss them in too. I add the powder and set the cycle on a ten-minute delay before racing up to my room. Thank God we're in officer housing, no more pesky trips to the laundry mat. The memory hits me all of a sudden—my first date with Ollie. As soon as it comes, I push it away, but the dull ache it brings lingers in my chest.

Slipping into my white bathrobe, I sit down at my desk with my cell, sending Dad a quick text. No matter how I write it, it sounds bad, so I settle for simplicity.

Dad,

Just wanted to let you know something weird happened tonight. I was down at the beach with Cole and

I frown at the screen, hitting the delete key.

with some friends and a kid from school washed up on shore. We called an ambulance, but it was already too late. Not sure how he got there (he wasn't with us) or what happened. I didn't really know him, but it's so sad. I'm ok, just wanted to let you know.

As soon as I hit send and sit back in my chair, I get a reply.

You sure you're alright? Do you need to stay with a friend tonight? I don't want you to be alone.

I frown. Dad and I have had a bumpy relationship for the past few years, and it's only just gotten better. I kinda hate lying to him.

I'm fine, but Cole offered to stay on the couch tonight just in case. Don't worry.

I hit send and chew on my thumbnail until he responds. Dad isn't Cole's biggest fan. Maybe the long hair and leather jacket have something to do with it. Maybe it's Cole's carefree, James Dean-esqe rebel vibe, or the way he's so completely comfortable around me that upsets Dad so much. Maybe it's just in Dad's genetic code to hate any guy I bring home.

Even from a thousand miles away, I can feel him frowning, torn between being glad I told him the truth and wanting to punch Cole in the face.

The reply finally comes. *I always worry. Be good. Lock your door.*

I laugh. *I will. Night. Love you.*

The reply is faster this time. *Love you too.*

I put the phone down and take a deep breath. The water has stopped, so I peek out my door just in time to see Cole cross into the living room in the T-shirt and sweats, drying his dark hair with a yellow towel.

Closing my door, I step into my own private bathroom. Technically, my room is the master suite of the house, but Dad reasoned that I have more stuff and therefore need more room—not gonna argue with that, though I think he was just being nice. My bathroom is decorated much like my bedroom, all violet and forest green. My bath mat is thick and fuzzy under my feet as I turn the knob to the shower.

The hot water feels good, maybe better than it ever has, as it works to loosen my tense muscles and wash away the grime matted into my hair. But I know the washer will be flipping on soon, so I force myself to make it quick. By the time I'm dried off, dressed, and have my hair dried, it's after four am. I cross into the living room to find Cole fast asleep as the TV flickers light across his face. Pulling up the blanket to cover him, I turn the screen off. He sighs and rolls over, tucking his face into the pillow. I stare at him for a minute, glad beyond words that he decided to stay.

I should go to bed, I know that. I should go to my room and lock my door. But I can't. The idea of being alone...

With a deep, resigned sigh, I go back to my room, gathering my pillow and blanket, and drag them to the living room. Curling up in the recliner, I close my eyes, the sound of Cole's breathing lulling me into a deep, dreamless sleep.

I **HAVE NO IDEA** WHAT TIME IT IS WHEN I FINALLY

wake up. The scent of fresh-brewed coffee rouses me, wafting through the air like liquid sunshine. Blinking, I see that Cole is gone from the couch, the architect of the coffee no doubt, and his blanket is folded neatly at the end of the sofa, pillow on top. I yawn, stretching and throwing my hair back in a hasty ponytail before heading for the kitchen.

"Morning," I groan, entering the room.

He looks up from his bowl of cereal and laughs. "Wow. Long night? You look like crap."

I glare at him. "Creeper."

He points to the coffee maker on the counter without looking up from his newspaper. "I installed java."

"Oh har-har," I respond, pouring myself a cup. The clock on the microwave reads 2:12. "Is it really after two?"

He nods as I take a seat across from him. "Yep. And I would still be asleep except the mailman rang your doorbell and woke me up. You got a package." He jerks his chin, gesturing to a small, brown box on the counter.

I retrieve the box, ripping it open. Inside, there is a large, white conch shell and a note.

Thinking of you.

Love, Oliver

I gently set it back in the box. My heart sinks in my chest, a dull, hollow feeling.

As if reading my mind, Cole takes a sip of coffee,

not looking at me when he speaks. "You two talk recently?"

I press my lips together. "Nope."

"Maybe you should call him, let him know you got it?"

I sit back, cradling my warm mug. He's right, I know that. It's time to hash things out, see where we stand. But somehow, I can't bring myself to do it. "Honestly, I'm kind of afraid to. I'm afraid the next time we talk, that will be it. It will just be over. I'm not sure I'm ready for that yet." I shake my head. "I know. I'm a terrible person."

He makes a *pfft* sound. "Please. If that were true, it wouldn't be bugging you so much. But," he hesitates, setting the paper down and lowering his chin, "I want you to know that whatever happens with you guys, I'll still be here. I'm not just here because Ollie asked me to look out for you. You're my friend, and I care about you. I'm not going anywhere."

I'm about to make a smart-ass comment, but it gets trapped in my throat. "Thanks," I finally manage. "That means a lot."

"Yeah well, don't get all sappy about it," he says, changing the subject. "In other news, it looks like they're ruling Mac's death a suicide."

I can't help the look of surprise on my face. He pushes the paper over toward me. I scroll to the headline: *Local Teen Takes Own Life*. There's no mention of Cole and me specifically, just a general statement that he was found washed up on shore after apparently jumping to his death earlier in the evening.

"It says he sent his parents a text before he died," I read, looking up to Cole, who is staring at me. "And according to them, he couldn't swim."

Cole nods. "They think he jumped off the pier earlier and had just washed to shore."

Something about that just sounds so bleak, so wrong. I hadn't known Mac well, but he never seemed the type. Hell, what do I know? I suppose under the right set of circumstances, anyone could be the type. Then something else occurs to me, something that makes me absently chew my bottom lip.

He raises an eyebrow, staring at me. "Uh-oh. I know that look. What are you thinking?"

I don't look up at him, taking a sip of coffee, my eyes fixed on the paper in front of me. "It's probably nothing."

He pulls the paper away, forcing me to meet his eyes. For a moment, I'm reminded of the first time we met, the day Oliver introduced us. I remember looking at his eyes and thinking that no one should have eyes that perfectly sky blue. His hair was shorter then; now it hangs at his chin when he doesn't have it slicked back. The sides of his head are shaved short, only the center stripe is long, allowing him the illusion of short hair when it's gelled back, or the illusion of long hair when he lets it fall to the sides. Some guys can't pull off the long-hair thing without looking like a girl. Cole doesn't have that problem. His face is far too masculine to ever make that mistake. His jaw is square, with a hint of dark, patchy stubble always present.

"Well, it's just that we jumped off the pier and the current pulled us down the shore. I mean, even swimming against it, we ended up probably a quarter mile right of the pier."

He nods. "Yeah? So?"

I shrug. "So why did his body wash up to the left of it? The current should have taken him the other direction."

He thinks about it for a minute. "Maybe he didn't jump from the pier at all. Maybe he went into the water somewhere else. Does it really matter?"

I frown. "No, I suppose not."

Cole sits back, folding his arms across his chest. "You really can't help yourself, can you?"

Without thinking, my hand finds the small, gold charm around my neck. It's a tiny spy glass—a gift from Oliver. He'd given it to me for Christmas after he'd been accused of arson and I'd gotten him off by finding the person who was really responsible. Since then, I've developed a bit of a reputation around the school. People come to me with everything from hacked MyFace accounts to stolen bikes. To say I do it for the cash would be untrue—though a little extra money in my pocket is nice. But at the end of the day, Cole is right. I really just can't help myself.

The ding of the dryer carries through the house. Cole must have switched it out when he woke up. I take another sip of coffee. "If you're going to do my laundry and make me coffee, I may never let you leave," I joke.

He grins widely, pushing back his chair and rising to his feet. "If the only reason you want me to sleep over is for maid service, you're using me wrong," he offers with a wink.

"You better quit flirting with me, Cole. What would Amanda say?" I ask. "Or is it Jenny this week?"

He hollers from the other room. "It's Courtney this week and don't worry. She's a sharer."

I almost spit my coffee out my nose. "Gross dude, TMI."

He comes back into the room, basket of clothes in hand. "Not like that, oh ye of dirty mind. I like Courtney. She's special."

Now it's my turn to raise an eyebrow. "Then let me ask you this—what is Courtney's last name?"

Cole's eyes widen, a look of absolute confusion etched on his face. The expression is so comical that I can't help but laugh.

"That's what I thought."

THREE

Monday morning, the entire school is buzzing with news of Mac's death. Grief counselors are holed up in the library, and there's going to be some kind of assembly. As I walk to first period with Kayla by my side, I can't help but wonder how someone who was so virtually invisible in life could be such a super star dead. It's as if anyone who ever said two words to him is now completely traumatized. People are crying, holding hands, and sniffling into huge wads of tissue.

It feels... weird. Especially considering I actually saw the body.

My best friend Kayla props herself against the door, appearing seemingly out of nowhere as usual. Her skirt is too short for school regs, so she's added some dark, strategically ripped tights under it. The gray shirt she's wearing is little more than scraps of cloth held together with a variety of safety pins and thick hot pink thread. As always, she's sporting black-and-white plaid suspenders covered in comical buttons saying everything from, "Save the Dinosaurs" to "Blog This". Her hair is bright pink this week and held back in two low pigtails, her thick bangs falling into her narrow, almond-shaped eyes.

"This sucks. We shouldn't have even had school today. They should have cancelled. No one is getting anything done anyway. Half the school is crying in the library." She pauses before adding, "I shoulda just ditched."

Kayla's especially bitter today, and it has little to do with the sour mood around school and more to do with the fact that her boyfriend, Derek, is off with his mother for spring break in Hawaii. Add that to losing a friend, even a casual acquaintance type of friend, and she's having a really shitty weekend. I look at her, pressing my thumb and index finger together.

"Do you know what this is?" I ask.

"The world's tiniest violin playing *cry me a river*?" she guesses.

"No. It's three-thousand compress pounds of I love you, and when you release it, it goes," I open my fingers, "screw those assholes."

She playfully slaps my hand, her armful of bangle bracelets clanging together. Next to her, I look downright conservative in my jeans and long-sleeve T-shirt. The only slightly colorful thing about me today is the strip of vibrant blue I've allowed her to put in my otherwise plain brown hair. From down the hall, Cole approaches, with the leggy, redheaded Courtney at his side. She kisses him on the cheek and breaks off, waving to us before heading to her own class.

"Hey," he says, leaning against the lockers.

"Hey yourself," Kayla says in a flat monotone. She turns to me. "I'll see you in class."

Brushing past Cole, she heads to her seat. It isn't that she dislikes Cole himself, but he—and Oliver's other friends—travel in a whole other social sphere than we do. For a while, I had been able, through my dating Ollie, to join the factions. But as soon as he left, things had gone right back to the way they were. The jocks at their table, and Derek, Kayla, and me at ours.

Sometimes, Cole will cross lines and sit with us, but not often. As a former football player and now soccer team captain, he's jock table through and through. But he also has just enough *rebel without a cause* going that he can slip into brooding outcast mode like changing a shirt. Though they're never rude or unfriendly toward me, I know all too well that my invitation to come behind the popular curtain has been revoked.

And I'm kind of fine with that.

"Do I smell bad or something? That girl acts like I have some kind of contagious disease," he complains.

"Neurosyphilis?" I joke.

He shudders. "That's not even funny."

"It's a little funny," I protest. "But no. It's not something you're used to, I'm sure, but she just genuinely dislikes you."

He scoffs at the idea. "Please. Chicks love me."

"Not to burst your bubble, but no, not all females are helpless against your charms."

He grins. "You love me."

I put a hand on his shoulder. "Yes, I do. But that might just be the neurosyphilis talking." The bell rings and I wave goodbye as I settle into my class.

Kayla leans over as the teacher begins taking attendance. "Please tell me you aren't actually falling for that."

I frowned. "What? For Cole? He wishes."

She twists one pigtail around her fingers. "Yeah, I think he does actually."

"Please, we're just friends. Besides, he is the biggest man-whore I know. I'm not stupid enough to fall into that pit, even if I did think of him that way—which I don't."

She just sits there, her expression smug. "Whatever gets you through the night, Farris."

Proceeding to fill her in on what happened Saturday night, I tell her about how it was Cole and me who found the body. I expect her to make some kind of morbid joke, but she just shifts uncomfortably in her chair. That's when I remember she actually knew Mac. He'd tutored her in computer science or something in her freshman year. Like me, he was a tech-head, really into game design and coding. I'd only ever met him once, in passing, and only now does that thought make me a little sad. We might have been friends, in another life. But Kayla had counted him as part of her little freak army all the same. I reach over and hold her hand. Normally, the teachers might say something about it, but today, they just ignore us.

CLASSES ARE A JOKE TODAY, AS KAYLA PREDICTED. Most of the kids are in the library, and teachers are just trying to hold it together with the few people who actually show up. By the time lunch rolls around, I'm so bored I'm seriously considering pulling a fire alarm, just for kicks.

Beside me, Kayla picks at her tofu and sprout salad. I opt for a slice of pizza and an energy drink. Even with the extra caffeine, I still feel like I'm about to fall over dead. A quick glance over my shoulder shows me all Ollie's friends at their usual table. The cafeteria is a Venn diagram of the worst kind, each clique arranged according to popularity, numbers, and, of course, wealth. The A-list jocks occupy the round tables nearest the back of the room; that's the football players, lacrosse, soccer, and basketball teams intermixed along with the cheerleaders and the pep squad. They are flanked on either side by the B-list jocks; that's your hockey, gymnastics, swimming, and track kids. Moving clockwise, we find the stoners, then the Goths, then the hipsters jamming out on acoustic guitars in the far right corner, followed by the junior ROTC crowd, who already move like mini-soldiers and are eyeballing the hipsters like they are about to storm the beaches at Normandy to get those guitars away from them. Between that table and mine are the real party people, the overachievers, many of whom are hunched over doing homework. Swinging my chin to my left, I follow the lines of tables, the art and drama kids, the hardcore gamers and nerds, and finally, the factionless, bridging the gap between those poor, cliqueless souls and the B-list jocks are the food lines. Before I know it, I'm staring at Ollie's table again, his still-empty seat mocking me. Even Courtney is up there, her back to me, but her hair an unmistakable shade of auburn. So needless to say, I'm extremely surprised when Cole scoots up next to me.

"Have I told you that you look like crap today?" he says, his face serious. "Did you not sleep at all last night? Because I can pull off tired-sexy, but on you, it's just sad."

I pick up my pizza with one hand and flip him off with the other. He chuckles.

"We can't all be sociopaths," Kayla chimes in,

glaring. "And shouldn't you be sitting with the cool kids?"

He shrugs, adjusting his jacket. "I don't think I would be very welcome today. Courtney and I had a falling out."

"Another one bites the dust," Kayla mumbles.

"What happened this time?" I ask.

He flinches. "She was under the impression I didn't go to the dance with her because I had to work. But I swear to God I don't remember telling her that. I swear I just told her I was busy. It's not my fault she inferred that to mean work."

I swallow a bite that's a little too warm and launch into a coughing fit. He waits for me to finish.

"Anyway, she felt bad about going to the dance without me, so she showed up at the restaurant to hang out with me. Pablo told her I had the night off..."

He doesn't need to explain further. The Pizza Shack owner is well known for his big mouth. "She found out you were with me," I finish for him.

He points to his nose. "She asked me about it today. I wasn't going to lie. Long story short, she took exception."

Kayla stabs at her salad. "I wonder why."

Cole sits back, looking genuinely affronted. "What's that supposed to mean?"

She doesn't look up as she speaks. "It means you use your friendship with Farris as a way to leverage yourself out of relationships. Something starts to get too serious for you, and suddenly, it's all Farris, all the time, until they break up with you. Basically, you're making Farris the bad guy so you don't have to man up and deal with your own shit."

I blink, too stunned to speak. I don't know if I've ever heard her say more than five words to Cole, but she just gave him a verbal smackdown in the middle of the cafeteria. If I wasn't so uncomfortable with the topic at hand, I'd be starting a slow clap. As it is, I'm just trying not to blush.

He rolls his eyes. "Yes, I know. I'm a terrible person. But no way was I going to let Farris spend the anniversary of her mom's death alone." His voice is a hoarse whisper as he swings his gaze from her to me. "And as for the rest, I never meant to make you the bad guy or use you as an excuse. You know that, right?"

"I know." What else can I say? Thank you doesn't seem like enough. But Kayla has a point too. He can't keep looking after me as an excuse for tanking his relationships.

"Don't worry," Kayla chimes in, her voice high with false excitement. "I'm sure there's some other big-busted, naïve wanna-be just waiting to pick up the pieces of your broken heart."

Cole smiles, holding up his hands, his fingers crossed.

I can't help but laugh. With a pat on my back, Cole stands up, shoves his hands in his pockets, and walks out of the cafeteria. No sooner is he gone than another unexpected visitor arrives. Courtney leans over me, her red hair almost falling into my tray. I look up, trying not to frown.

"Hello, Courtney. Is there something I can help you with?"

Her face is flushed, her lips pressed into a thin, angry line. "Just wondering—how long *was* Ollie gone before you moved in on his best friend?"

I feign shock at her words. Actually, I'm surprised there aren't more expletives in the sentence. But hey, the conversation is young. "Come on, Courtney. You know very well there's nothing going on between Cole and me. If there was, he would have found some excuse to dump *me* by now."

She actually snarls. "So what? You're like, playing hard to get to keep him around? That's just pathetic."

I sigh and turn to face her. She backs away just a bit. Smart girl.

"No. What I'm saying is that we are *friends*. That's all. Cole is fiercely devoted to his friends, like Oliver and like me. But he treats his girlfriends like used Kleenex. Case in point."

She puckers, looking a bit taken aback by my words.

I continue. "Look, you knew his reputation when you met him. And maybe, deep down, you hoped you could be the one to change him. But in my experience, love doesn't change people. It just makes them even more who they really are. You knew who and what he was going into it. So don't come over here looking for someone to blame for getting your heart broken. That's all on you."

Courtney stands up, looking like she wants to slap me. Holding her gaze, I don't back down for a second. I watch as the decision forms on her face, and she walks away.

"That boy is bad news," Kayla says, absently shoving food around her plate with a fork.

I wholeheartedly agree, but part of me can't help but wonder if he might just be worth it.

After last period, I walk out to my car. Lucy, my beautiful, gunmetal-gray '67 Mustang Shelby Fastback sits in the parking lot, shining in the afternoon sun. I lean against the driver door, waiting for Kayla to meet me so I can give her a ride home. A small piece of white paper flaps in the breeze, drawing my attention to where it's tucked under my windshield wiper. I snatch it before it can blow away. Probably a lame flyer or party invite, I think, opening it up. Scrawled in thick, black marker across the page is a message so strange that I have to read it twice.

It wasn't a suicide.

There's no name or anything else on the paper. Just those simple words. In the back of my mind, something flares to life. The nagging feeling I had before is back and stronger than ever. Mac hadn't jumped off that pier. Whatever happened, someone besides me knows it wasn't suicide, maybe even knows the truth about what really went down that night.

And they want me to figure it out.

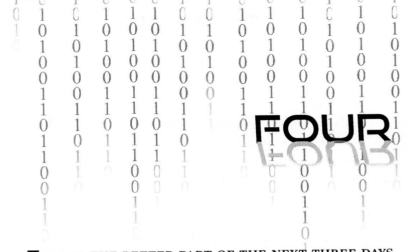

FOUR

I SPEND THE BETTER PART OF THE NEXT THREE DAYS systematically hacking all of Mac's social media accounts—which turns out to be a challenge. Not only was he tech savvy, but he was also deeply paranoid. By midnight on Wednesday, I'm at my wit's end. Other than a few fragments of messages and a handful of clap-chats, there's not a scrap of anything that gives me a clear picture of just who he was, or what he was into. There are only a few photos of his dog, a Pomeranian named Betsy, and his used Honda Civic. I rub my eye, slumping to the side in my desk chair just as my phone vibrates.

It's a text from Cole.

Where you been, Bueler?

I frown. I haven't been avoiding him, not exactly. But it's hard not to think about the things Kayla said. When I don't text back immediately, the phone buzzes again.

Seriously, you ok?

I text back. *Fine, just working on something.*

His response is fast. *Just finished my shift. Want me to bring over some pizza?*

I grin. Since Cole gets to take home any botched orders at the end of the night, the chef, Mario, always screws up at least one order. Pepperoni, pineapple, and jalapeño. My favorite.

If I ever say no to that, shoot me because an evil robot has taken over my body.

He sends back a winkey face and I gently toss the phone back on the wooden desk, folding my arms across my chest.

He arrives at my door in less than ten minutes, large pizza in one hand and a six-pack of apple soda in the other. Opening the door, I grab the pizza and soda and then close the door in his face with a laugh. He opens it as I turn my back to him and walk the food into the kitchen, setting it on the counter.

"Haha. Very funny. I see how it is." He pauses, eyeing the blue folder on the table. "What is this?"

I jerk my head, motioning for him to take a peek. "I got a note on my car Monday after school."

He winces, the unopened file in his hand. "Not Courtney, I hope. Sorry about all that. Didn't mean to put you in the middle."

"No. It wasn't Courtney; at least, I don't think it was. The note is in the file, top page."

As he skims the file, I plate up some pizza, crack open two sodas, and flop into a seat beside him, scooting one of the glass bottles his way.

"What does it mean?" he asks finally, leafing through the pages.

I sit back, swallowing the lump of lukewarm pizza in my mouth before answering. "Someone wants me to look into Mac's death. Which means someone in that school either knows what happened, or knows the police got it wrong. And they want me to figure it out."

He looks up. "If somebody knows something, why not go to the police? Why come to you?"

I shrug. "That's a question I'd love to ask them, but first I have to figure out who left the letter."

Shaking his head, he looks back down at the file. "And this is going to help how?"

"I'm trying to figure out who his friends were, who he hung out with. It's a place to start at least. Friends might know if he had problems with anybody or if something was going on in his life."

He frowns, raising an eyebrow as he looks back up at me. "Is this a copy of the police report?" He flips the page. "And the coroner's report?"

I take a sip, not meeting his eyes. "Maybe."

"And you got it how?"

"Would you believe me if I said they just left it laying around?"

"If by laying around, you mean it was on their computer, then yes."

I shrug again. "Not my fault the police department uses outdated, glitchy software that anyone with a sixteen-digit pass key cipher can just walk right in and take a look at."

Finally, he closes the file, taking a seat beside me at the table. "You are a terrifying creature, you know that?"

Popping a slice of pepper in my mouth, I grin.

"So, any thoughts so far?" he asks, taking a long drink.

I wipe my hands on my jeans and grab the file. "Actually yes. I found something... here." Flipping to the page, I spin the file back to Cole.

He looks at it like it's another language. "And this is?"

"Best I can tell, it's a receipt for a personalized domain and hosting. But I couldn't find a site attached to his name."

"Any way to tell what kind of website?"

I shake my head, taking the file back and closing the cover. "Nope. Not without accessing his computer or his tablet. And odds are good that they are both sitting in his room."

Cole narrows his green eyes suspiciously. "I feel a favor coming on."

"My best chance at getting some quality alone time with that computer is during the funeral Saturday. And I could really use a lookout."

"And Kayla..."

"Is going to the funeral. I don't want to say anything about this until I know for sure there's something to say. She was his friend, one of very few, I think."

He nods, playing with the now-empty soda bottle. "Understood."

"Thanks. In the meantime, I'm going to access the counselor's files and see if any of the students have been feeling particularly chatty or broken up about his death."

He shoots me a look of mock disdain. "I see both your loose morals and your bad taste in pizza and I'm judging you accordingly."

"Judge away," I say, helping myself to a second slice.

THE NEXT DAY AT SCHOOL, I NEARLY FALL ASLEEP IN AP European history. My study partner Tasha kicks me under the desk, making me jump.

"Yes, Miss Barnett?" Our teacher, Mr. Henry, points to me.

I have only a heartbeat to scan the notes on the projector behind him.

"Who were Austria's allies during the Seven Years' War?" he repeats, and I exhale deeply.

"Russia and France," I answer and he turns away, clicking the remote to move to the next slide. Turning to Tasha, I mouth, *Thanks*.

By lunch, Derek and Kayla are both genuinely concerned.

"Seriously, are you sick or something?" Kayla asks for the third time.

I shake my head. "I'm fine. Just not sleeping well, not since..." I trail off. Not since I found Mac's body washed up on the beach.

"You can stay with me," she offers, leaning her back against Derek.

Plucking the Red Bull off my tray, I gently shake it. "No thanks. I just need another one of these."

As if on cue, Cole falls into the seat beside me, setting a bottle of iced lemonade in front of me. "That's it, you're on decaf," he says with no preamble, swiping the can from my fingers.

I raise one eyebrow. "Traitor."

"I brought you something from my trip," Derek chimes in, digging in the inside pocket of his pinstripe vest before holding out his hand to me. I cup my palm, and a fragile, silver chain spills out into my hand, a mother of pearl-encrusted shell hanging on the slender rope.

"Wow, it's amazing," I say, clutching it in my fingers before slipping it over my head. "Thank you."

"What, nothing for me?" Cole jokes.

Derek raises one black, polished finger. "Actually..." He pauses, digging in his pocket, producing a tiny box and handing it to Cole. "Here, this is for you. I wasn't sure if you already had it, so..."

Cole is genuinely taken back, and Kayla sits up, clearly shocked by the gesture. He opens the box and pulls out a small, glass tube, shaking its contents. "What is it?"

Derek's mouth turns up, twitching once before he answers. "Crabs."

It's two full beats before I realize the joke and descend into uncontrollable laughter. Beside me, Kayla is laughing so hard she's clutching her stomach and gasping for air. Derek is grinning, but he still looks pensive, as if he's just not quite sure how Cole is going to take it.

For his part, Cole just shakes his head. "The gift that keeps on giving. And it's not even my birthday." Finally, he smiles and Derek visibly relaxes.

In my pocket, my phone vibrates. There's no name, but I open the text anyway.

While you're screwing around, someone is getting away with murder.

I feel the muscles in my neck and back immediately tighten.

Who is this? I text back.

The message comes quickly. *Doesn't matter.*

I text again, this time closing my eyes against the noise of the cafeteria, straining to hear the familiar ding of a text tone. *Why come to me? Why not go to the cops?*

Then I hear it, and my eyes swing to the A-table across the room. I can't be sure, but I think it came from somewhere over there. My phone vibrates again.

Don't look for me.

I frown, listening again to be sure. *Why not?*

This time, there is no sound as whoever it is probably turned off their ringer. I'm still convinced it came from somewhere in that corner, but when I turn to look, I don't see anyone on their phone. My phone buzzes again, however.

Because I didn't do it.

FIVE

BY THE TIME COLE PICKS ME UP SATURDAY MORNING, I have a mental list of items to look for and a handful of excuses prepared just in case I get caught breaking into Mac's room. Tossing my backpack on the floorboard of his black CRV, I crawl in.

"Good morning, sunshine. You ready to rock this B&E?" he asks, pulling out of my driveway.

Winding my hair around my hand, I create a bun at the back of my head and affix it with the rubber hair tie on my wrist. "You make it sound so exciting."

He doesn't look at me as he speeds through a yellow light. "Please. It's just another day at the office for you. But for some of us, it's a first time. Can you blame a guy for wanting to make it special?" He pauses. "Did you bring ski masks or something?"

Now I shoot him a look of exasperation. "One, no, because it's broad daylight and that's a little conspicuous, and two, you are staying in the car, parked across the street where you can watch the house, so you can warn me if someone comes home early."

Now he looks at me, grin wide. "So you're saying I'm the getaway man."

I roll my eyes. "I'm really going to regret this, I can tell."

We pull up outside the two-story townhouse and park across the street. Luckily, the funeral is being held off base, so the family and most of the neighbors have already gone. The street is quiet. Pulling my bag onto my lap, I unzip it, checking one last time that I have everything.

"How are you getting in?" Cole asks, surveying the street.

Digging into my pocket, I pull out a simple cut key. "Bump key. I just push it in the lock and then tap it with this while I turn it." I hold up a rock from the bottom of my bag. "It's not the most sophisticated thing, but it'll work fine. All these places have older locks anyway, and no one will ever know it happened."

"And you know this how?"

I shrug, dropping the rock back in the bag. "Looked it up online. I swear to God you can learn absolutely anything on YouTube." When I look up, his expression isn't one of confidence. "Relax, I practiced on my lock at home to get the hang of it. It'll work."

With that, I slip into a pair of tight-fitting latex gloves and open the door, tossing the bag over my shoulder and stuffing my hands in the pockets of my gray hoodie, leaning through the window before I go. "I'll call you and leave the line open on speaker, so if you see someone, you better tell me ASAP. If someone comes in, I will get out through the back second-story window and go around the block. Drive around and pick me up."

He salutes. "Got it, boss."

Nodding once, I shuffle across the street. Stepping up onto the porch, I reach out and ring the bell before shoving my hand back into my jacket. I want to be sure the place is empty before I go busting in. As I stand there waiting, I glance down and see something familiar. As I pick it up, I shake my head. It's one of those fake rocks you hide keys in. I turn it upside down and sure enough, there's a key inside. I use it to open the door before returning the key and rock to their original positions. As soon as I'm inside, I close and lock the door behind me and dial Cole, putting him on speaker and sticking the phone in the breast pocket of my flannel shirt.

"So much for the bump key," I mutter, taking stock of the house. Knowing I don't want to be in here any longer than necessary, I skim the house, moving from room to room until I finally see a far door with a toxic waste symbol plastered across it. "I think I found his room."

Pushing the door open, I creep inside and close it behind me. There's a window, but it's covered with heavy blackout curtains. The room itself is clean, but cluttered. Books, piles of video games, and computer components are all stacked in neat piles on every surface. The closet door is open, displaying a poster of Einstein sticking out his tongue and a rod full of T-shirts. The laundry basket is empty. Narrowing my eyes, I move to his tall dresser and slide open the top drawer. Folded in neat squares are piles of socks and underwear.

"Well, I think Mac had a touch of OCD. Wonder if he was on meds," I say, thinking out loud. A dry grunt is the only sound from Cole.

Scanning the room, I see his computer, a beast of a machine, on a desk in the far corner of the room. The screen is a forty-five inch LCD monitor, the tower large enough to operate a power plant. Taking a seat, I drop my backpack at my feet and boot it up. Immediately, the green screen demands a password. Pulling a USB from my bag, I plug it into the tower and back into the startup screen, running my decryption program. While it runs, I continue my search, pulling open desk drawers and finding nothing but homework and study guides.

Something catches the corner of my vision, a charging cord running from the outlet behind the computer, along the base of the wall, and ending...

Under his mattress. Rolling the chair across the carpeted floor, I slide my hand under the mattress and grab the tablet, pulling it into the light. "Hello, beautiful."

Sliding it on, I'm surprised to find there's no passcode set. For a minute, I debate just taking it, but decide better of it. If the family knows it's here and it winds up missing, well, that could look very bad for me. On the other hand...

Grabbing my bag, I pull out my own tablet and set to work.

"What is taking so long?" Cole demands.

"It's not a smash and grab, Cole. I'm spoofing his tablet."

"You're doing what?"

"Spoofing. Cloning. I'm downloading a copy of everything from his tablet and putting it on mine. Of course, I'm going to lose all my stuff, but I have it backed up so I can restore it later. In the meantime, anything on his tablet, I will have access to."

Across from me, the computer finally completes its reboot, and the password is accepted. The desktop image glows to life. It's a selfie shot of Mac and another familiar face snuggling on what looks like this very bed.

"Hey Cole, I'm gonna put you on FaceTime," I say, hitting the button on my cell and facing the camera at the screen. "You know this chick? She looks really familiar."

"Yeah, that's Ashleigh Cassel. She's dating that ROTC dude. Cody, I think his name is."

Of course, that's why she looks familiar. "She's

in my history class. She's always talking about how her boyfriend has his pilot's license and how he takes her up in the plane sometimes."

I don't know much about Cody, but he, like the other guys in his clique, seem at least outwardly very stern, very serious. Behind me, the house phone rings, and I nearly jump out of my skin. "Shit," I say, clutching my shirt. "I think I just had a heart attack."

"Enough playing around. You need to get out of there; I can't take the stress," Cole says, trying to joke, but ripples of tension fill his tone, betraying him.

"Ok. Nearly done."

Sliding another USB, a blank one this time, into the tower, I begin copying files. I do one more sweep of the room while it works, but I end up with nothing but an inhaler and a stack of unopened condoms.

Ten minutes later, I manage to get out of the house unseen. Once I'm back in the car, I strip off the gloves and shove them in my bag, sliding out the tablet and opening it up.

"Where to now, my felonious friend?"

"Back to my place," I say, not looking up.

BACK AT MY HOUSE, COLE SITS AT MY DESK, COMBING through the files I've uploaded from Mac's computer. I sit cross-legged on the floor, my back against the wall to his left, examining the tablet.

"I need food," Cole says finally, spinning the chair to face me. Glancing up at the clock behind him, I realize that it's after six and we skipped lunch.

Lowering my chin, I shake my head. "I told you, no food till you find something."

He narrows his eyes and I sigh, throwing my hands up. "Oh, fine. I'll order pizza, but only because I don't want you calling OSHA on me."

I try to stand, but my legs have gone numb from sitting so long and I pitch forward. The tablet slips from my hand as I reach forward to catch myself, knowing in that heartbeat I'm about to go down, hard.

Moving so fast I don't even see it, Cole steps forward, lunging from the chair and catching me mid-fall. He pulls me to standing, and I fall against him like a rag doll. When I look up, he's smirking. I only have a moment to process the sudden closeness, the feel of his arms around my waist, clutching me to him, before he speaks.

"You know, I've had girls throw themselves at me, but I've never had a girl literally throw herself at me before."

I try to step back, but my legs won't obey. I have no choice but to let him continue to hold me. "Keep dreaming, Cole McAllister," I challenge. He gradually lowers his face, and I'm paralyzed. His smirk falls, replaced with something else, something... primal.

At that moment, the pain hits and I squeal.

"Ahhh! Pins and needles. Pins and needles." I writhe in his arms and he finally scoops me up, the sensation making me cry out again, and deposits me into my desk chair.

"You try to recover sensation in your extremities, I'll order the pizza."

When he leaves the room, I'm torn between wanting to laugh and wanting to cry. For a second there, I really thought he might kiss me. The idea makes me shiver. I push the thought away. There's a million reasons why it would be a terrible idea, a million reasons it was wrong, a million reasons it should never, ever happen.

But is there a reason why it should?

No sooner has the thought surfaced than he pokes his head around the corner. "You want breadsticks too?"

I can only nod.

When he vanishes again, I exhale, slumping forward onto the desk, looking at the screen for the first time. The USB took over three hundred files from Mac's computer—photos, eBooks, notes, emails, but what catches my eye is a file labeled Omega.

When I click on it, a file opens, some kind of spreadsheet. Alias on one column, dates on the next, followed by three sets of what seems like random numbers, then finally a row of Xs and Os.

"Cole, I think I found something," I holler, and he

strides back into the room.

"What?"

Motioning for him to look at the screen, I explain. "There's this place on the deep web called Omega Portal. It's like, a black market internet site. This file was called Omega. Could be a coincidence, but I doubt it." I stare at the screen. "These are usernames and dates, but I can't figure out these three rows."

He leans back. "I've seen something like this before. You got a newspaper?"

I nod, getting up to go grab one off the stack in the garage. Dad has a subscription, too old school to get his news online, and with him gone, I've been tossing them straight in the recycle bin. "Here," I say handing him the most recent one.

He sits at the desk, opening the paper to the sports section. "That's what I thought. This number is the spread, the total points scored. Look, this date refers to the Michigan State versus Notre Dame game. That's the point spread, 41-26. Then that is the bet, and the last number must be the win or loss. See, some numbers are negative. And the Xs and Os are probably whether it's been paid or not."

I stare at him in disbelief.

"What? I can't know stuff too?"

I can't help but smile. "You're a genius. You know what this means? He was running an illegal gambling ring, probably on the Omega Portal. I can use these user names to track down the domain."

He claps his hands, then rests them behind his head and leans back in the chair. "My work here is done."

Turning, I scoop the tablet off the floor, silently thanking my lucky stars it wasn't damaged in the fall. "So why would he have it on there and not on here? He was clearly a tech head. He'd want it to be portable, but I can't find anything but some funny videos, a calendar, and some music on here."

"Maybe it's in the calendar?"

I pull open the calendar. Sure enough, there are some regular entries, but not games. "These entries are all the same. Mondays and Thursdays at five pm, base library," I say. "Guess we are going on a field trip."

"To the library?" Cole whines. "Worst field trip ever."

"If you're right about that gambling ring—"

He cuts me off. "And I am."

"Then assuming that Xs are paid and Os are open accounts, there's going to be someone looking to get paid. If he didn't have the cash to cover and someone found out he was the man behind the curtain, it's a very good motive for murder."

Cole squints. "Not really. I mean, you can't get blood from a stone—or in this case, a dead guy. My money's on the girl. It's always about a girl."

Much as I hate to admit it, he's got a point. "I'm

still leaning toward money, but we'll dig in both directions and see who hits pay dirt first."

The doorbell rings, and he's out of his chair like a shot. "Pizza's on me."

"Who says chivalry is dead?" I call behind him as I go back to playing with the tablet, the nagging feeling I'm missing something playing in the back of my head like an out-of-tune violin, constant and annoying.

SIX

THE LIBRARY IS SLOW, NOT THAT I EXPECTED A packed house at eight o'clock on a Friday night, and despite the bright overhead lights, it's eerily quiet. The entrance is a long hallway where local painters' works are displayed on the walls. This month it's bright, Piccaso-esque abstract canvases. Beautiful, raw images that remind me of someone trying desperately to make himself heard but not knowing quite what to say. When we finally spill out into the central room, the librarian's desk is empty. A self-service kiosk sits on the far side of the desk, a scanner on a mechanical arm for checking books in and out attached to a touchscreen monitor.

I take a deep breath, smiling. "You smell that?" I whisper.

Cole sniffs the air. "Desperation? Loneliness? Nerds?"

"Books," I say, running my fingers along a shelf of classic poetry. "One of the best smells in the world."

"How can a girl as tech friendly as you not prefer

eBooks to print?"

"The same reason you only listen to jazz on vinyl. Digital is nice, but nothing compares to the feel of a spine in your hands, the paper and leather and fabric. It enriches the experience."

He nods in understanding.

Just as we reach the end of the row, a young woman pushing a metal cart barrels into Cole, nearly taking him and the cart to the ground.

"Oh, I'm terribly sorry. I didn't hear you come in. Is there something I can help you find?" she asks. Unlike the stereotypical buttoned-up librarian, she is probably in her mid-thirties, thin but not overly so, with a simple red cardigan and jeans. Her blonde hair hangs in loose waves around her face, framing her thick lips and wide, gray eyes.

"Do you work Monday nights?" I ask, earning myself an exasperated look.

"Yes. Why?" Her tone is curt as she pushes the cart past us and we have to walk behind her.

Cole holds up his hand to me in an *I've got this* gesture. When she stops to shelve the next stack of books from the cart, Cole hands them to her one at a time, offering her a hint of a smile. "Our friend usually hangs out here on Monday nights. I was wondering if there was a book club or something that night?"

I watch her meet his eyes, and despite the massive age gap, I see her expression soften, a light blush rising to her cheeks, and I have to fight back a gag. Turning my back to them, I pretend to be interested in something on the shelf in front of me.

"No, book club is Wednesday at seven. The only thing we have Monday night is kids' story time. Oh, and a few people have the private room reserved for tutoring sessions. The schedule is on the door."

"That must be it then," he says, and I can feel him behind me, leaning in closer. "This is him."

Glancing over my shoulder, I see he is showing her Mac's desktop photo, the one of him and Ashleigh, on his phone.

"Oh yes. They are in here every week."

"They? He was tutoring her?"

She nods. "French, I believe. Though I know he tutored in computer science too, or at least, he used to. I haven't seen him with anyone but her in months."

He leans back. "Cool. Thanks."

As we walk out of the stacks, she yells, "Book club on Wednesday if you're interested."

Cole turns, waving and smiling, before turning back to me.

"Wow, that was impressive," I offer, shaking my head.

"What?" he asks, opening the door.

I spin, walking backward into the parking lot and pointing toward the building. "You and her. The mountain lion."

"I think you mean cougar."

Making a clawing gesture with my hand, I swipe at him, "Rawr. Whatever you say."

He points to me. "We shall never speak of this again."

I make the clawing gesture again and he lowers his chin, shaking his head.

"Mind if I crash at your place tonight?" he asks as we get into my car.

I give him a once-over before turning the key. "You know, at some point, you are gonna have to get used to this guy being around."

He shrugs. "Or I could just kill him."

The engine of my rebuilt Shelby roars to life. "You do realize prison orange is not your color, right?" I say, not looking at him as I pull out of the parking lot. Its full dark already and the street lamps halo in the early evening fog.

"I'm serious though, this guy... there's something off about him. I don't trust him. I really don't want him in my house."

When I glance over, I see his eyes are fixed on the road ahead, his jaw ticking as he clenches his teeth.

"I still think it's in your head. I mean, face it, you would feel that way about any guy your mom brought home, but if it'll make you feel better, I can look into him for you," I offer.

When his eyes meet mine again, the relief is

plain to see. "Yeah. That'd be great. Thanks."

I shrug. "Least I can do for a guy who threw himself at a leopard for me."

He chuckles. "Cougar."

I shrug and turn on the radio.

I DON'T REALIZE I'M SCREAMING UNTIL COLE SHAKES me awake and I can feel the last sounds dying in my throat, which is raw and sore.

"Are you okay?" he asks, sitting on the bed beside me. "Jesus, it sounded like someone was murdering you."

Sitting up, I reach over and flick on my bedside lamp. My arm muscles ache and a light sheen of sweat covers my skin. "Just a bad dream," I say, raking the mess of damp hair back from my face.

"You wanna talk about it?" he asks, leaning back on one arm. "I hear if you talk about a reoccurring dream, it goes away."

I shake my head. "Tried that. A year of therapy and nothing to show for it."

"Try again."

I look him in the eye for the first time, and see his expression is still, waiting. There's a patience in his crystal-blue eyes that puts me at ease. Taking a deep breath, I begin. "It usually starts in the hospital. Before Mom died, she was hooked up to all these machines. I was always so afraid I'd trip on a cord or lean on a tube and accidentally kill her. So I look down, watching my steps so carefully, and when I get to the bed and look up, she's gone. It's just empty. I try to back out of the room, but the door is locked. All this water starts rushing in from under the door..."

Closing my eyes, I take another deep breath. "Sometimes, I drown. Other times, I'm running in this maze of corridors, looking for her while the water rises around my feet. Sometimes, other people are there, sometimes, it's just me and I can feel my heart pounding so hard I think I might actually die. But it always ends the same, with the water overtaking me."

He sits quietly for a moment before speaking. "You have nightmares about drowning, and you thought it'd be fun to jump off a dock into the ocean in the middle of the night?"

"I thought it would help me get over it," I admit with a shrug.

He leans over, nudging me. "That's my girl. Always doin' the dumb thing."

I half grin. "It might have worked, except for... Mac."

His smile falters. "I know. I'm having a hard time keeping it out of my head."

Leaning forward, I pull my knees up and rest my chin on them, rubbing my face with my hands. "I have to figure out what really happened to him. I might never sleep again if I don't."

Reaching out, Cole strokes the side of my head. The gesture is both comforting and oddly intimate. "We will. I promise." He looks at me for a long minute, and then stands, offering me a hand. "Since I doubt either of us are going back to sleep now, how about I make some coffee and we can get back to work?"

Taking his hand, I let him drag me out of bed. I grab my tablet on the way to the kitchen, tinkering with it as he brews a pot of light roast.

"Still think there's something on that?" he asks, retrieving two mugs from the cabinet.

"There must be something I'm missing. His tablet was top of the line; I'm talking the kind of money that would mean selling a kidney in Mexico. No way he buys that much machine and only uses it to keep dates and watch cat videos."

"He was probably afraid to keep anything on it in case his parents found it."

My head snaps up. "Of course."

Opening the settings on the tablet, I finally see what I missed. A secondary log in. I tap the tiny icon at the bottom and the screen goes dark, then, green text appears demanding a passcode.

"Of course what?" Cole asks, taking a seat at the kitchen table beside me.

"He had a dummy front. If his parents opened it to snoop, this is all they would find. The rest of the contents are hidden behind a secondary user account. It's password protected, but I think I can get past it."

Ripping open a box of pop-tarts, he slides a foil package my way. "You gonna brute force your way in?" he asks.

I look up at him and crinkle my nose. "Look at you, learning all the jargon and stuff."

The side of his mouth turns up in a lopsided grin. "Can't help it, you never. Quit. Talking."

"Fair enough. But no, I'm probably better off to come up with a work around. I have a program I can run on it that might do the trick. It'll take a few hours at least."

"That's cool. I work this afternoon, lunch shift, but I'm off at four. You wanna meet up then?"

I sit back in my chair, tearing open the silver wrapper and sliding out the cold pastry. "What, no hot date tonight?"

As he leans across the table, his eyes lock onto mine. The expression on his face is serious. Something about it makes my heart leap into my throat and stick there. Just when I'm sure he's about to do something—say something—he lunges down, snaps a bite of the pop-tart in my fingers, and winks at me. "Nope. No hot date, just hanging with my best girl, trying to solve a murder so she can sleep again." With that, he rises from the chair and turns his back to me. "I've heard that sleep deprivation can make your brain do all sorts of nasty things. You might start hallucinating, or join the young republicans or something."

With a snort, I snap myself out of my momentary daze. When I turn to face him, he's already gone, disappearing down the hall to the bathroom. I turn back in my seat, staring at the chunk of missing pastry in my hand, wondering what the hell is the matter with me. I don't have a full minute to wonder why Cole's closeness has put me in such a state before my phone rings. Picking it up, I feel my heart drop in my chest, guilt hitting me like a cartoon boulder.

Oliver.

I debate letting it go to voice mail, but I can't bring myself to do it. "Hello?"

"Hey Farris..." He hesitates, stammering. "How's it going?"

His voice is unsure, and I don't realize why until I glance over at the counter and see my phone charging near the toaster. I must have picked up Cole's phone by accident. Shuffling my feet, I shift in my chair. The pastry falls from my other hand, and I wipe my fingers on my pajama pants. "Oh you know, same old same old. How are things on the island?"

"Wet, mostly. It doesn't really rain, but it's like a constant mist in the air."

I force a smile, only to remember he can't see it, so I let my face fall, leaning forward on my elbows. Silence crackles between us.

"So, where's Cole?" he finally asks.

My eyes flutter closed, and I take a breath before answering. "He's in the shower, getting ready for work." I quickly add, "It's not what it sounds like."

Another long pause.

"I know," he says. "Is it wrong that it still bugs me? I mean, I know I asked him to look out for you, but..."

My mouth twitches. "Yes. No. Maybe a little?" I sigh. "He's been going through some family stuff and with my dad gone, I've been so freaked out since we found that body, it's been nice not to be alone." My mouth clamps shut as I realize I hadn't mentioned Mac or what happened that night until now.

"Cole told me what happened. I'm sorry I can't be there," he offers. I exhale, glad I hadn't accidentally dropped a major bomb on him. "It's just the idea of him being there for you when I can't... All these thoughts go through my head, him holding your hand or wiping away your tears, or even just sitting beside you on the couch—it's killing me and it's not even real, I know that. I know neither of you would do anything... but still. I would be there if I could. You know that, right?"

Standing, I pace to the far side of the kitchen and lean against the wall, resting my forehead on the smooth plaster. Cole had done all of those things with me—for me. It's not just his imagination; I feel it too. Entire days go by when I don't even think of him anymore. And despite my best efforts... "I know I just..." I trail off, gathering my thoughts, steeling myself to speak the words I've been avoiding for weeks. "I just didn't think it would be this hard."

There's a long pause this time, neither of us wanting to speak. It's the feeling of dread. You see something terrible about to happen, but you can't stop it. You can't even move. That's how I feel in this moment. Paralyzed.

"Maybe it shouldn't be," he finally says.

There it is. The hammer dropping, the crushing blow, the inevitable defeat. It feels like something dying inside me. "Maybe not," I say, my voice squeaking despite my best efforts.

"If I asked you..." He hesitates, taking a deep breath. "If I asked you to stop hanging out with him, would you do that?"

The question catches me off guard. Would I? Would I stop hanging out with Cole to make Ollie feel better? The real question is, could I?

"No," I say with all honesty. Cole being around is more than a convenience. He, more than anyone else in my life right now, is my rock, the person I lean on the hardest. And I know he needs me too. Maybe not in the way Oliver fears, but it's there, it's real, it's strong, and I'm not willing to give that up. "I need him. I think... we need each other. I'm sorry, Ollie, I know that's not what you want to hear, and I wish, I wish things were different."

"I know. Me too." He pauses before adding, "I still miss you. Whatever happens, just be careful, ok?"

The first tear slips from my eye, and I don't even try to wipe it away. "Goodbye Ollie."

"Bye Farris."

Rolling around, I press my back against the wall and let myself slide down. My chest tightens until it's nearly impossible to draw breath. Waves of nausea roll through me, and I know if I'd eaten anything, it would be coming right back up. I pull my knees up to my chest and curl into a tight ball, letting the tears fall. I don't realize I'm shaking until I feel a steady hand on my back. I turn my head to the side, seeing Cole through the blur of moisture in my eyes.

"How much of that did you hear?" I ask with a sniffle.

Squatting down, he sits beside me. "Enough." He leans over, wrapping one arm around me. "You didn't have to do that." His voice is gentle, softer than I've ever heard it, almost a whisper.

Blinking away the tears, I raise my chin, holding his gaze. "Yes, I did. I need you. And not just on this case, but... in my *life*." Something flashes in his eyes, and I realize I've said something wrong, freaked him out. Stuttering, I continue. "I don't have many friends, even fewer that I can really count on, and I'm not willing to give you up. I'm sorry; I know that's selfish of me."

He squeezes me closer. "You know, I've never had anyone need me, not really. And for what it's worth, I need you too." He pauses, shaking his head. "Which is also a first for me. What a fucked-up pair we make."

I laugh, and my whole body shakes. "Tell me about it. And aren't you breaking some kind of moral code here? Bros before hoes or something?"

Releasing me, he stands and offers me a hand up, which I accept. "Well, that would imply that you're a ho, and make no mistake, I wouldn't be here if you were."

I know he means it as a compliment, but I *feel* like a ho. Relationship ruiner, heartbreaker, wedge driver, pathetic loser. "So what am I then?" I ask jokingly.

His face falls, the kidding washed away and replaced by something I can't quite place. My heart skips a beat in my chest, and I realize I'm holding my breath. As quickly as the expression comes, it's gone, replaced with a cocky half-grin.

"You're the chick who's going to run to the store. You're out of bar soap in the shower."

I turn my back to him, going for my keys on the counter beside my still charging phone, and maybe trying to give myself a moment to recover the look of half relief, half disappointment that is probably scrawled all over my face like graffiti on a train. "Use the shower gel."

"And smell like flowers and rainbows and unicorn farts or whatever the hell you girls like to smell like?" He makes a *pfft* sound and heads back down the hall, leaving me alone in the kitchen, keys in hand. I don't move again until I hear the bathroom door click closed.

Deciding to grab soap at the nearby convenience store rather than drive all the way to the Commissary, I get home just in time to hear the shower turn off. I set the tiny package, too late to do any good, outside the door, grab a cup of coffee, and head to my office. Syncing my computer to the tablet, I wirelessly download the malware and start it on the tablet. It's designed to go in and launch a password reset rather than try to figure out the original password. With as careful as Mac was, he probably installed a dead man switch on the tablet, three incorrect password attempts and the whole drive would delete itself. I have something similar on mine, and I don't want to risk it.

Sitting back in my chair, I pull one knee up to my chest and blow across the steaming cup of coffee while I check my email. Cole walks in, hair wet but combed back, his bright orange T-shirt with the pizza parlor logo sprawled across the front clinging to his well-toned chest. Circling me, he puts his hands on the back of my chair and leans forward, so close I can feel the heat radiating off his skin.

A mix of emotions floods me, the first of which

is the warm blush of relief I get when he's close, then a strange twisting in my stomach, then guilt, then sadness, and then anger at the sadness. A rush of feelings tugging my insides this way and that. I take a deep breath, forcing my mind to be still, and say the only thing that comes to mind.

SEVEN

"**Y**OU SMELL LIKE UNICORN FARTS," I SAY, NOT looking at him.

He straightens, lifting an arm and sniffing himself. "Damn it, I knew it."

I grin behind my mug. "Relax. In twenty minutes, you'll smell like grease, sausage, and tomato paste. No one will ever know your dirty secret."

He grunts, and then spins my chair so I'm facing him. "You sure you're ok? I can call in if you need me." He playfully wags his eyebrows. "And I know how you *need* me."

I take a sip of coffee with one hand and flip him off with the other.

He puts a hand on his chest. "Oh, what? Are we done talking about our feelings now? Or should we braid each other's hair or something?"

"Go to work, Cole."

He salutes me, then spins on his heel and heads out, leaving me to the soft hum of my computer and my gnawing self-doubts. Memories of Ollie and me float through the empty space in my mind. Oliver is probably the last bona fide romantic on the planet. He always held my books and walked me to class; he brought me flowers and he danced with me even when there was no music. Most weekends, we ended up on picnics, team barbeques, or hanging out at the beach. He made every moment, no matter what we were doing, feel like the whole world revolved around us. But my favorite moments were the quiet ones, when it was just us, sitting on my bed, reading, talking, or playing checkers. He had one of those smiles that was boyish and full of optimism, and yet, was somehow still incredibly sexy. He made me feel like anything was possible. I close my eyes, trying to remember his kiss, what it felt like when his fingertips brushed the hair from my cheek right before his lips touched mine. But it's gone. All I have now are flashes of memories, slivers of feelings. I open a file on my computer and scroll through all the pictures of us together. My insides ache as I look at our smiling faces staring back at me.

He made me happy, that much was undeniable. And he never said or did quite what I expected him to. Being with him—loving him—had been easy, like breathing, something I did without even thinking about it. But then, I remember watching him drive away, he and his sister Georgia in his truck, boxes piled into the bed. I didn't cry until much later, but when I did, it felt like goodbye, like part of me knew it was already over. Who falls in love at sixteen anyway? That's just stupid.

I shut the folder and set down my coffee, opening and starting a quick background search on Elliot Mede, Cole's mom's new side guy. He's a staff sergeant with VMAQ 120, born in Michigan, enlisted at nineteen. I scroll down his reports, looking for any red flags, and then shoot it off to the printer in the far corner of the room, perched precariously on top of an old, red milk crate. Aside from one drunken bar fight in A-school, the dude looks solid. Divorced once, three years back. No kids. No police reports or felony convictions. Just a stack of service commendations and a handful of photos pretty typical of a single guy screwing off on deployment.

Basically, if I were auditioning a new dad-type, this guy would make my short list.

A loud chime breaks me from my thoughts. The tablet is showing a reset password prompt. I quickly type in my own password, and the screen comes to life. There's a digital spreadsheet, which looks like a record of the bets and payouts from his little enterprise. There are also files full of code—I'll have to dig through each to figure out what their specific purposes are—and there are a huge amount of locked files. The mp4s are easy enough to open, but some of the text files are encrypted.

"Damn Mac, paranoid much?" I mutter to myself, launching a bot to break the encryptions.

While I'm waiting for that to run, I open the first mp4 and it's Ashleigh Cassel, lying on her back on Mac's bed, her yellow hair splayed out like a cartoon sun around her head. She's making faces at the camera.

"This is so boring," she complains, glancing off screen.

Mac answers off camera. "If you weren't so afraid to be seen in public with me..."

She laughs and blows a kiss at the camera. "Please, if Cody knew about us, he'd kill you."

Mac comes into frame, the back of his head blocking the camera. "Maybe that's a risk I'm willing to take," he says, and the video freezes into a still shot as he leans forward, I assume to kiss her. Most of the videos are similar, Mac and Ashleigh screwing around in his room. One is a decently steamy make-out video shot from an angle that makes me wonder if she even knew it was being recorded.

I scan through them quickly, and then open the message files, scrolling back through thousands of late night texts. Reading them makes me feel like a Peeping Tom, looking through the window at the most private moments of their lives. Taking my coffee, I relocate to the couch and curl up. Honestly, I'd been expecting a bunch of adolescent drama at best, sexting at worst. But this, this was somehow both more and less than that.

I just don't understand why you let him treat you

like that. You are better than that.

You don't understand. In my family, status is everything. Appearances are everything. My dad has been having an affair for 3 years and Mom knows. But she won't file for divorce because she doesn't want to lose her lifestyle.

Is that how you really feel?

I feel worthless. Unless I'm with you. You are the only person who sees me.

Then further on.

Madison isn't eating solid food anymore. She's on an all-juice diet. She's dropped like 6lbs.

Pretty sure that's anorexia, not a diet, lol.

Whatevs. She just wants to squeeze into that dress in the window at Nordstrom's. She's a 6 trying to be a 4, you know?

That reminds me. Did you tell him about us yet?

I tried, but it's complicated.

Try harder.

K. I'll tell him after the spring formal.

WHY AFTER?? I thought you wanted to go with me?

I do, but he already rented the limo and everything. Besides, it will be better in public, trust me.

I'M NOT SURE AT WHAT POINT I DRIFT OFF, BUT THE sound of my front door slamming closed wakes me up and I jolt upright, the tablet sliding to the floor.

"Christ, you scared the shit out of me," I grumble at an equally startled Cole.

"You? You damn near gave me a heart attack." He reaches back out the door. "I brought you a present."

I glance up at the clock before getting up. Ten past four—even with the coffee, I'd slept the day away. "What is it?" I ask right before he walks in, clutching a giant whiteboard.

He rolls his eyes. "It's a murder board."

Now I feel dumb. "A murder board?"

He heads down the hall toward my office. "Grab the other pieces out the back of my car."

I obey, bringing the two metal feet and assorted brackets in from his trunk.

He produces a screwdriver from the depths of his Swiss army knife and begins the assembly. When he's done, the board stands about six foot tall, and it's on wheels. He stands back, admiring his work, then glances at me.

"Um, thanks?"

Pulling a blue marker from his pocket, he steps forward and draws a line. "A murder board helps you track a person's last-known whereabouts, so you can figure out who the last person to see him alive was."

I have to admit, I'm impressed. It's a little old school, but a good idea for sure. "Where'd you learn all this?" I ask.

"Don't you have cable?" he asks, not looking

back at me. He draws a dot at the end of the line and makes a line perpendicular to that, writing *body found*, and the time we'd called the cops.

"Of course I have cable. What do I look like, a cave man? But police procedurals aren't really my bag."

Finally looking back to me, he hands me the marker. "Don't know what you're missing."

"So we retrace his steps. We know he was at the dance, because of the tux."

He holds up a hand. "Not necessarily. He may have been taken out before he got to the dance. We need to find out if anyone saw him at the dance, what time he was there and when he left if so."

"And how he got there; he didn't have a car, if I remember right."

He nods. "And if he didn't have a car, how'd he get to the beach?"

I tap the cap of the marker on my bottom lip. "And I think I know just the person to ask."

"Well, that's going to have to wait. Because this fabulous murder board is less a gift, and more a bribe," he says, taking a step back.

"Oh really?"

"So, my mom is basically demanding I go to dinner with her and Elliot tonight," he begins, frowning. "And I was hoping you'd come too. Well, that's kind of putting it mildly. Basically, there's no way in hell I'm going in alone."

Handing him back the marker, I smile, "Is it safe to assume that to forego this meal would mean getting another murder board, with your name on it?"

"It is."

"Well then, how can I refuse?"

ON THE WAY OVER, I FILL HIM IN ON THE RESULTS OF my search. He says nothing, but his hands clutch the steering wheel so tight his knuckles are white. I'm not sure if he's relieved the dude is clean, or if he were hoping for a validation of his distrust.

Cole's house is cozy, an off-base townhouse not far from the main gate. Since the breakup, his dad has kept the enlisted residence, but once the divorce is done, he'll be back in the bachelor's quarters. I've been here enough times that his mom's taste in classical furniture and baroque design no longer seems out of place. The soon to be ex-Mrs. McAllister is a classy lady with a job as manager of the local credit union. She's actually a little Stepford for my tastes, never a single hair out of place, always looking like she stepped straight out of a *Glamour* magazine. Still, she's friendly, relaxed, and hard not to like. Then again, I've also seen her fly off the handle and turn into some kind of four-foot-eleven Tasmanian devil in high heels, so, there is that.

Cole hesitates outside the door for just a

moment, shooting me a pained grimace before throwing the door open. "Ma? We're here."

Mrs. McAllister steps out of the kitchen with a spatula in one hand and a wide smile across her face. She's in black slacks and a tan blouse with a lavender-colored apron covering most of her front. Part modern business woman, part nineteen-fifties housewife. No wonder Elliot was smitten.

"Farris, I'm so glad you could join us for family dinner tonight," she says, crossing the room to hug me. Turning to Cole, she smiles, but I watch as it falters just a bit around the edges at his expression. His jaw twitches like he wants to say something, but he holds it back.

"Please be nice to Elliot," she whispers, brushing her hand down his T-shirt sleeve.

He sighs deep. "I'll try."

Spinning on her heel, she leads us into the kitchen where Elliot is setting the table. He looks up at us and hesitantly smiles. He's in nice jeans and a polo shirt, only his shaved head betraying his career choice.

Being a staff sergeant in the Marine Corps might not pay well or be glamorous, but it is honest work, the kind of work you do when things like honor, integrity, and duty actually mean something to you. Lord knows there are easier ways to make a buck.

"Farris, right?" Elliot asks, holding out his hand. "I've heard a lot about you."

"All lies and defamation, I'm sure," I say, shaking his hand across the table.

He chuckles. "You sound like your dad."

Cole gently nudges me toward a chair, and then rounds the table to grab a salad bowl without a word to Elliot.

The three of them set the table in the most uncomfortable silence I've ever witnessed in my life, each carefully maneuvering around the others so as not to accidentally make contact. Once everyone is all seated, I hastily fill my water glass from the pitcher.

"So," I say, trying to break the silence. "How is life over in 120?" I ask Elliot before shoving a bite of lasagna in my mouth.

He frowns. "How did you know I was at 120?"

My hand freezes halfway to my mouth. *Motherfu—*

"I mentioned it," Cole says in an offhand way, not looking up from his plate.

Glancing over at his mother, I see her stiffen. I've never seen a parent with such a well-honed bullshit detector. "Is that so?" she asks, her tone even.

Finally, he looks up, his expression unrepentant. "I asked her to run a background check on you," he says, looking Elliot square in the eye.

"You can't be too careful these days," I say weakly. "People run checks on babysitters and stuff all the time. I think he just..."

"Wanted to make sure I'm not a murderer?" Elliot interrupts, seeming unfazed.

"I think he was just looking out for his mom. Honestly, I'd do the same thing if my dad ever started dating again," I say, steadying myself.

Elliot waves it off. "I assume I came out clean?"

Cole stabs a chunk of tomato and stuffs it in his mouth, not answering. Elliot turns his gaze back to me. "Lucy tells me you are something of a computer whiz."

"I think that might be overselling it a bit, but I'm competent," I say, taking a drink.

"I hear you helped shut down the hacker who brought down that plane last year," he continues. "That's a helluva accomplishment."

I mutter a thanks and scoop another forkful of food into my mouth. The cheese is stringy, and I can't get it to break off. Beside me, Cole snickers. I shoot him a pathetic look and he takes mercy on me, snapping the cord with his fork.

"So, how long have you two been together?" Elliot asks.

I swallow quick enough to respond in unison with Cole.

"We aren't together."

He smiles. "That's a shame. You're cute together."

Cole sets his knife and fork on his plate, leaning forward. I'm sure he's about to say something that will send his mother into fits, so I kick him under the table. He turns to me for a moment, and then back to Elliot.

"She's way out of my league."

I chime in. "That's true."

"And she's way too smart to date a guy like me."

"That's also true," I agree. He gives me the side eye. I innocently bat my eyelashes.

"And she's way too mental for me. I like my girls more low key."

I shake my head. "That's not true at all. That's the opposite of true."

We manage to get through the meal with a minimum of dirty looks and finally, halfway through dessert, the dam breaks.

"So, are you like, living here now?" Cole asks just as Elliot takes a bite of blackberry pie, nearly choking on it.

His mom is the one who responds. "Perhaps this conversation is best had later."

Cole swishes the ice in his glass around before pointing a finger at Elliot. "If you mean when the guests are gone, then he probably shouldn't be here either."

Just when her face turns a shade of red I'm pretty sure precedes a nuclear explosion, Elliot covers her hand with his own. She visibly relaxes.

"I'm not living here, but I stay most weekends, and I come over after work most nights to spend time with your mother, and with you if you'd ever come home," Elliot says, his tone level, but with a warning in it.

Cole sets his glass down. "You know she's still married, right? Isn't there some sort of rule against dating married women?"

"Cole!" his mother snaps.

"Your mother was free to date whomever she wanted as soon as the papers were filed. I'm sure she explained the state makes you wait six months before the papers are finalized."

"Still, kind of crass, isn't it? Swooping in before the ink is even dry on the paperwork?" Cole says, his voice rising.

I open my mouth before I can think better of it. I want to tell him that sometimes there is no mourning period for a relationship, that sometimes, you can develop feelings for someone without meaning too. But I don't get the chance. His mother pipes in again. This time, her voice is tight like a rubber band stretched too thin.

"At least I waited until after we separated!" Standing, she throws her napkin on the table and storms off toward the living room. Elliot gives Cole one last unfriendly glare, and then follows her.

Cole sits there, probably as stunned as I am.

Did his dad really cheat on his mom? It wouldn't be a huge stretch; fidelity was tough when you often spent months, sometimes years, away from each other. Hell, I couldn't even make it three months in a long-distance relationship. Even so, that was one hell of a blow to level.

Beside me, Cole is red-faced, staring down at his food, his hands balled into fists on either side of his plate. Standing, I begin gathering plates and make my way to the sink. Behind me, the telltale clinking of glasses tells me Cole is following suit. Plugging the left sink, I run water, full hot, and squeeze in a gob of lemon-scented bubbles.

"I'll wash," Cole offers, handing me a dry dishcloth, which I sling over one shoulder.

From the other room, we hear raised voices and Cole walks over in slow motion.

"He shouldn't have to find out like that." Elliot's voice rises above the sound of running water.

"I'm just so sick of Cole treating you like the enemy when he doesn't even know the truth. And it's not like David would ever come clean with him."

Shutting off the water, I go back to the table, stacking the last of the dishes before moving to Cole's side in the archway leading to the living room. In the reflection of the gilded mirror hanging above the banquette, I see Elliot, his arms wrapped around Cole's mom, swaying gently while stroking her back.

Leaning against Cole, I slide an arm around his waist and whisper, "Everyone needs someone."

He looks down at me, a tic working in his jaw, and nods once before pressing a soft kiss to the side of my head. "Come on, let's get this done."

Turning back to the kitchen, he scoops up the stack of plates and dumps them in the soapy water, scrubbing each before setting them in the adjacent sink for me to rinse, dry, and stack.

"You know, I'm feeling like I got the short end of this deal," I mutter, rinsing a plate under the cool, running water.

Without warning, Cole scoops up a handful of bubbly dishwater and tosses it at me, splattering across my blue tank top.

"Hey!" I say, pulling the wet cloth off my skin.

He doesn't look at me when he responds. "Geeze, Farris, watch what you're doing."

Narrowing my eyes, I take hold of the sprayer head and point it at him, letting loose a torrent of water. He tries ducking and then wrestling me for control of the hose, but it's no use, I've got a ninja death grip on it. We manage to cover each other, the counters, and the floor with water before he finally releases my hands and opts to just shut off the tap.

"I wondered how long it'd take you to figure out to do that," I say, tossing the hose in the empty sink.

Without warning, he grabs me around the waist. I try to wriggle free and my shoe slides on the wet floor, sending me falling backward. Cole tried to stop my fall, only to lose his own footing, and we both go down. He lands half on top of me, knocking the air from my lungs. In that moment, something inside me snaps. Suddenly, I'm not in the kitchen anymore. I'm in another room, with another boy, only he's pressed over me, one hand tearing at my clothes. The memory hits me so fast that all I can do is scream.

EIGHT

JUST AS SUDDENLY, I COME BACK TO MYSELF. COLE IS on his knees, scrambling off me, dragging me to a sitting position while holding onto my hands as I struggle to get free.

"Farris, Farris, its ok. Everything's ok. You're here. It's me. It's Cole," he's repeating over and over, trying to calm me. Shaking, I feel my arms relax and I let him draw me into the circle of his arms. His mother is beside us, her voice worried.

"Did she fall? Is she ok?" she asks.

I clutch Cole's T-shirt, wishing I could tell him not to say anything, not to tell them what a freaking wreck I really am.

"She's fine," he says, holding me. "We were screwing around and fell, but she's ok. I think it just surprised her," he says, helping me to my feet. "I'm gonna give her a ride home."

By the time I'm on my feet, I'm mostly recovered, except for feeling like a total moron. "I'm fine; I'm so sorry. I didn't mean to scare anyone," I say, wiping my face.

Pushing past Cole, his mom hugs me tight, one hand petting the back of my head. "It's fine dear. Don't worry about us. I just want to make sure you're alright."

I let myself be held, just for a moment, as I squeeze my eyes closed. It's not as good as a hug from my own mother, but it's very close. Some kind of maternal pheromones that make you believe that, as long as they are there, everything's going to be all right. I don't get that very often, so I soak it up. When I pull away, Cole offers me his hand and leads me out the front door. I wave a quick goodnight, but I don't really relax until I'm in the car, door closed, seatbelt on.

"You sure you didn't hit your head or something?" he asks, heading back to the base.

I roll my eyes. "No, I'm fine. Trust me, I've had enough head injuries to know."

He's quiet for a moment. The wind streams in through the window, caressing my face, tugging at the damp strands of hair, chasing away the last slivers of nervousness from my freak-out. "Oliver, he told me what Reid did, that he hurt you. I didn't know how bad..." He trails off.

"He didn't," I snap defensively. "He didn't... *hurt* me. He tried to, but he didn't." I cross my arms over my chest, part of me angry that Oliver said anything about the incident. If I wanted the world to know how damaged I am, I'd wear a sign. I glance over, and his eyes are laser fixed on the road. I sigh. The idea of Cole thinking I was... that I'd been... it is nearly unbearable.

"When we fell, it knocked the wind out of me. I don't know why I went there in my head. It was just, kind of a reflex or something. I dunno," I fumble, trying to explain.

"PTSD," he offers.

I frown. "I don't think it's anything that bad. It's not like it's happened before. It was just this once."

"Do you think it will happen again?" Now he looks at me, and his expression is so full of concern that I have to look away.

"I doubt it. I've just been so stressed out," I begin.

He cuts me off. "I'm sure my personal drama didn't help matters. I'm sorry."

Reaching across the seat, I hold out my hand. Taking one hand off the wheel, he laces his fingers through mine. "Don't be sorry. It wasn't you or your family or anything like that. It's just the piles of trauma inside my own head. Nothing you can do about that. But honestly, just being here helps. It helps a lot," I admit.

Squeezing my hand, he offers me a challenging grin. "Well, I'm not going anywhere."

"Noted, though you should probably stay at your own house tonight. Maybe have a heart-to-heart with your mother."

He makes a face. "Trying to get rid of me already? I see how it is."

Releasing his hand, I lean out the window. The air has shifted and now the promise of coming rain hangs heavy in the sky. When he drops me at my curb, I slide out of the car just as the first raindrops begin to fall. Walking deliberately slow down the sidewalk, I hit the front door just as the rain begins to pound the earth. Looking back, I see Cole, waiting to watch me go inside.

Everything I told him was true. I'm not sure when it happened, but I've grown to need him—far more than I should. Everyone needs someone, but that's the problem, the greatest tragedy in life. Because the people you need most are usually the first ones who leave you.

I'M UP BEFORE THE SUN MONDAY MORNING, DRESSED and in the school parking lot early. Tablet in hand, I make a beeline for the area where Cody and the other ROTC guys park. When he pulls up in his light gray Mercedes, I can't help but roll my eyes. I don't care how rich his daddy is, there's no excuse for a guy his age driving a car like that. Ashleigh pours herself out of the passenger seat, her blonde waves glinting in the sunshine.

I rush up to her, eyes wide. "Ashleigh, right?" I flip open the case on my tablet and plug in my password as I talk. "I'm so glad I found you. Mrs. Harris is being a beast about that stupid French test, and I totally lost my notes. She said you might have the notes for unit fourteen?"

She looks at me blankly, her sunglasses obscuring most of her face. "I'm sorry, what?"

I hold out the tablet to her. "Unit fourteen? Here, this section."

She glances down and her glasses slide down her nose, revealing an expression of near panic before she looks back up at me. I take the tablet back, closing the file of text messages. "So do you think you could help me? Maybe we could meet up during lunch?"

She recovers in a flash, glancing to Cody, who is greeting his friend Justin, and then back to me. "Sure. Meet me in the auditorium at eleven thirty. I'll bring my notes."

I press my hands together as if in prayer. "Thank you so much; you're a total life saver."

Before she can say anything else, I'm walking back up to the building. A familiar voice calls my name.

"Farris." Kayla slides up beside me, her purple and blue hair plaited in perfect pigtails. "What the hell? You don't call me all weekend?"

I grin, pulling the door open. "I figured you and Derek had some catching up to do."

She slides through the door, and then blocks

my path, "Is that all, or did Captain Skeezy finally sneak his way into your pants?"

I roll my eyes. "For the millionth time, it's not like that. I'm..." I hesitate. I had been about to say I'm with Oliver. Only that's not true, not anymore. "I broke up with Ollie," I admit, leaving her slack jawed as I pass her and head to my locker.

"Hold up, what happened? I thought you guys were like, rock solid."

She leans against the locker beside mine, picking at the hem of her mesh sleeve. As per usual, she's barely covered, the dress code being her own personal pincushion. Her plaid skirt is way too short, only the leggings underneath making it passable. The T-shirt over the mesh top barely covers her navel and hangs off one shoulder.

"I dunno. Just distance and stuff, I guess. It was just getting too hard. We were barely talking and..." I trail off, not wanting to admit the rest, but she, of course, guessed anyway.

"And he was pissed about all the time you're spending with Cole."

I frown. "Not pissed, exactly, but yeah."

Derek slides up beside us, planting a big, black lipstick-smeared kiss on her cheek. "It's easy to let insecurity get the best of you when you're not around to see what's really happening," Derek chimes in. I wave at him in a *thank-you* gesture, but he continues, "However, if he could see the way Cole looks at you, he'd have put a fist through his face weeks ago."

I scratch my eyebrow. "Ok, less than helpful."

Reaching out, Kayla takes me by the shoulders. "Look, you gotta either go for it, or shake it off. This in-between shit isn't good. Not for either of you." She jerks her head to the right, and I turn to see Cole talking to Courtney at her locker. She flips her long, red hair over her shoulder and laughs. At that, he takes her hand and they walk down the hall together.

And just like that, yesterday's vomity feeling is back. Maybe it's better this way, I decide. Maybe I just needed a reminder of the type of guy Cole really is.

With a scowl, I turn back to her, brushing it off as best I can. "Doesn't matter, because I spent the weekend digging, and I found some serious shit. I can now say, with confidence, that I don't think your friend Mac killed himself. I think he was murdered."

Kayla's mouth drops open before she snaps her fingers. "See? I knew it. I knew he wouldn't do that."

"Ok, so spill," Derek orders. "What'd you find?"

"You two come by the house after school and I'll fill you in, in the meantime, can you ask around and see if anyone remembers seeing him at the Spring Formal? Times would be great." Kayla nods, and I turn to Derek. "And can you see if anyone you know knows anything about a schoolwide internet gambling site?"

He gives me a flat look. "Not exactly my area of expertise, but I'll put out some feelers."

"Thanks."

Together, we head for first period, and I try really hard not to look at Cole and Courtney kissing outside the door as we pass by.

NINE

A SHLEIGH IS ALREADY WAITING FOR ME WHEN I GET to the auditorium. The red curtains are closed, and she's perched on the edge of the stage, her long legs dangling over the side, swaying gently so the heels of her tall, brown boots click the wooden risers below.

"So how much is this gonna cost me?" she asks, her chin up, staring at the lights above.

I set my backpack beside her. "What's what going to cost?"

Swinging her head, she glares at me. "How much is it going to cost to make those texts go away?"

My mouth twitches. Ashleigh is one of the few girls in this school who can afford designer instead of knockoff, thanks more to her mother's family money than her dad's JAG paycheck. Sure, it's not as much as he would make as a civilian lawyer but its damn close. Her grandpa is the current senator for our lovely state, and everything about her screams *money*, from her diamond earrings to her Prada

93

shoes.

"I don't want your money, Ashleigh."

Her expression narrows. "Then what do you want?"

Hopping up beside her, I mimic her pose. "I want to talk about Mac."

For a moment, her expression softens, hints of real pain cracking through the carefully painted surface, but she looks away.

"Well, you've read the texts, so you probably know everything," she says, her voice taut.

"Did anyone else know about the two of you?" I ask. "Like Cody?"

She shakes her head. "God no. Cody would not have handled that well, not at all." She pauses, looking back at me. "Why are you asking me all this?"

I level a gaze at her, searching her eyes for recognition as I speak my next words very carefully. "Because someone left me a note, telling me to look closer at his death. And I did. I don't think he killed himself. I think he was murdered. And I think someone saw it happen."

She blinks, clearly shocked, leaning away from me just a bit. Then she shakes her head, wiping away tears that haven't quite fallen yet. She sniffles. "No, that's not possible. Mac killed himself, and... it's my fault."

I take a deep breath. "What do you mean, it's your fault?"

Rolling her eyes, she answers. "He showed up to the dance. He wasn't supposed to come, we were going to meet up later, but he came anyway. He cornered me, told me I had to break things off with Cody or else he'd tell everyone about us." She sniffles again. "He made a sex tape. Did you know that? Of him and me. God, it would kill my parents..." She presses her lips together, looking at me with pleading eyes. "He did that kind of stuff. He used to joke that he knew everyone's dirty secrets. I thought it was funny, until... anyway, I told him we were done. I told him if he released the tape, I'd say he drugged me and..." She trails off again, but I can fill in the blanks.

"You'd say he raped you," I finish for her. She nods. My expression must betray my disgust because she defends herself immediately.

"I know how fucked up that is, but I just panicked." She wipes her eyes again. "And those were the last things I ever said to him. That's why he killed himself." Leaning over, she cradles her face in her hands. I don't hear her cries, but her body shakes with them.

Reaching out I rub circles on her back. "What happened isn't your fault," I say in a gentle tone. "And for what it's worth, I really don't think he killed himself."

She looks up, black streaks under her eyes. "Why? Because of some note? It was probably just a sick joke."

I shake my head. "There are other things too. If I'm wrong, then nothing changes, but if I'm right, shouldn't someone pay for what they did? Doesn't he deserve justice?"

Looking at me blankly, she answers. "Yeah. If someone hurt him, I want them to pay." Righting herself, she digs through her purse, retrieving a small box of wet wipes and a mirror. "What do you need to know?" she asks as she begins erasing the evidence of her tears. "What can I do?"

"What time did Mac get to the dance?"

She puckers, reapplying her lip gloss before answering. "A little after nine, I think. That's when I saw him at least."

"And when did he leave?"

She tilts her head to the side. "I'm not sure. I didn't see him after the argument, so it must have been soon after."

"And where was Cody?" I press.

She sighs. "Cody was at the dance all night. He drove me home after."

"What time was that?"

"Midnight. The dance ended at midnight." Packing away her makeup, she hops off the stage, turning to look at me. "I know what you think, but there's no way Cody would have done this, ok? He didn't even know about us, and I'd like to keep it that way."

"I'm not going to say anything, and once this is all over, I'll find that video and destroy it if you want. Just answer me one more question."

She nods.

I lick my lips, trying to find the most delicate wording I can think of. "Why Cody? What makes him a better boyfriend than Mac?"

"Cody is... stable. He knows where he's going in life. Air Force Academy and then public office. He has it all planned out. Mac, he was a wild card. Sure, he was quiet in public, but there was this renegade vibe to him. Being with him felt reckless, you know? A little dangerous."

"Mac was your Marilyn. I get it."

Nodding once, she turns on her heel to leave.

"Hey, one more thing," I call after her. "Can I see your phone?"

With a shake of her head, she digs it out of her pocket, handing it to me. "I guess. But I already deleted all the messages and stuff."

"I'm just putting my number in here, in case you think of anything that might be useful."

I enter my number, and then quickly install a phantom app I designed, a bit of malware that will let me access her phone at any time. I will need to get a look at her tracking info, just to rule her out. Switching it off, I hand it back. "Here you go."

THE PIZZA ARRIVES ONLY MINUTES BEFORE DEREK and Kayla. Her parents finally broke down and got her a used sedan that backfires like cannon shots every few blocks. I promised to help her fix it up, though honestly, that is more my dad's area than mine. He'd been a mechanic in high school, before deciding to go into the Corps, and it's still one of his favorite hobbies. As I carry the stack of hot cardboard into the kitchen, I sneak a glance at the calendar on the wall. Circled in thin, red marker is May twenty-ninth. The day he's slated to get home from his deployment. Just three more weeks. I can't decide if the time's gone by quickly or far too slow.

I'm setting out paper plates and red Solo cups, when the door opens, Derek and Kayla striding in.

"We come bearing beverages," she announces, entering the kitchen with two six-packs of Mountain Dew held at head level. "It's your favorite, the weaponized kind with the ginseng."

I take a pack from her. "Bless you tiny, caffeine-bearing goth-fairy."

"I brought presents too," Derek chimes in, handing me a folded piece of paper. Setting the soda down, I take it. "It's that website you were looking for."

I unfold the paper and stare at the hastily scrawled web address. "Awesome, thanks."

"Just as a heads-up, if you are considering entering into a life of illegal gambling, I'm told the site's defunct."

Fanning myself with the paper, I grin, "Well, we'll just have to see about that."

Reaching up, Kayla rubs her hand across my chin. "You've got a little evil on your face."

Slapping her hand away playfully, I motion to the pizza. "Fuel now. Menacing society after."

Each of us grabs a box and takes it to the table, taking our standard seats.

Derek taps the top of his box. "Why'd you get Mario's? Their crust tastes funny."

I roll my eyes. Before I can say anything, Kayla—who clearly knows me entirely too well—chimes in.

"Cole is working tonight, and she didn't want to risk him answering the phone." She turns, looking at me in accusation. I stick out my tongue.

Opening his box, Derek takes a deep breath, wafting the smell to him with one hand. "I suppose this will do then. But you gotta get this mess sorted out, cause I can't live like this for long."

Giving him the side eye, I open my box. The pepperoni, pineapple, and green pepper pizza is hastily tossed together, the cheese overlapping the crust on one side, leaving the other side with a thick strip of just sauce. I frown. Derek takes a bite of his bacon and sausage slice, making a dissatisfied face. Kayla raises one eyebrow before sinking into her extra-cheese-only pie.

"So," Derek begins, pausing to swallow a bite,

"what did you find out about Mac?"

Leaning forward, I put my elbows on the table. "Well, the guy had dirt on half the school. He was running an illegal gambling website, and he was screwing around with another man's girl. Basically, anything he could do to make himself a target, he was doing it."

Kayla stares at me, her pizza hanging half out of her mouth. "For real?" she mumbles around the bite.

I nod. "All that and probably more. He had some encrypted files in addition to everything else. I just cracked them today, haven't even had time to go through them yet."

"Well, the people I spoke to said they saw him at the dance around nine, but that he didn't stay long," Kayla says, wiping the corners of her mouth.

"I never did ask," I begin, getting up to grab three sodas before sitting back down and distributing them. "How was the funeral?"

She pops the top with a hiss. "Depressing, as a funeral should be."

Derek leans back. "Man, when I go, I want a bag piper at my funeral. I want people drinking and cheering and talking about how awesome I was. None of this doom and gloom."

"Oh, not me," Kayla says. "I want full drama, like a Mexican soap opera. People should be wailing and falling to their knees."

I reach over, taking her hand. "I promise that if you die before me, I'll cry at your funeral. I'll wear a giant, black hat with a veil and throw myself on your casket."

Beside her, Derek snorts, "Yeah right. There's no way you're outliving us. You eat like an unattended toddler, you drive like a swarm of bees flew in your window, and," he motions to the room around us with one finger, "you're always getting mixed up in crazy shit like this."

I take a bite, letting that sink in before raising my pizza slice into the air. "Touché."

By the time we are done eating, there's barely enough pizza left to cobble together half a pie, so we consolidate the boxes, grab fresh sodas, and head for my office. My fancy new murder board is set up in front of the far left wall, easily visible from my desk. Opening the small closet, I grab out two fluffy, black bean bags and toss them on the floor.

"Sorry, still working on the guest furniture thing," I say with a grin.

Kayla plops into one, her black lace skirt puffing up with the breeze she creates. "Suits me just fine."

Derek sidles up beside me, examining the board. Taking the marker, I begin adjusting the already made time line. It's a single line, the dot at the end being the time his body was discovered. "We found him at a little after midnight Sunday morning. Cole made the 911 call at twelve-nineteen, according to the police report."

I draw another dot at the beginning of the line with an intersecting line. "Ashleigh says she saw him at the dance at a little after nine, which is right according to the other witnesses." I scribble *dance @ 9:15 aprox.* on the intersecting line.

Turning, I grab a manila folder off my desk and open it, flipping through the pages. "Police say the text he sent his dad came in at ten forty-five pm." Balancing the folder in one hand, I make another dot. "That's the so-called suicide note. But it could have been sent by anyone. They never recovered the phone; cops think it probably went into the water with him." I hand the file off to Derek and make a note about the time.

"How did you get the police report?" he asks.

I don't look at him. "I asked very nicely?"

Kayla snorts. "She hacked in."

I turn back to her. "I liberated it."

"Don't suppose you could liberate that speeding ticket I got last month?" she asks, her tone light.

"And deprive you of the very valuable lesson about not speeding through school zones? What kind of friend would that make me?"

"The kind that doesn't get her eyebrows shaved off at the next sleepover?" she retorts.

I relent, holding up my hands. "No promises, but I'll see what I can do."

She blows me a kiss.

"So, the coroner puts time of death between ten and midnight. That's *super* helpful," Derek mutters.

"I know. But we have something they don't."

"Your keen and penetrating mind?" he asks with a grin.

"His tablet," I say, holding up the device.

"Where did you get that?" Kayla asks, lifting herself from the bean bag and taking the tablet from my fingers.

"I've been getting my vitamins," I say, taking it back.

"Would those be vitamins B and E?" Derek asks.

I point to my nose. "It's actually just a copy. I spoofed the real device. Now this is an exact copy of all his files. Took me forever to get through all the security. Your boy was seriously paranoid."

She shrugs. "Is it really paranoia if they are, in fact, trying to kill you?"

Derek and I nod in unison.

"Yeah."

"Pretty much, yes."

I hand the tablet to Derek. "Let's start by making a list of everyone he had dirt on. If he was trying to blackmail someone, that's always a good motive. I'm going to go look at the website. If it's really defunct, then someone shut it down. Since the guy running it is dead, I'd like to know exactly who that was."

"What about me?" Kayla asks.

"I printed out some maps and tide charts." I

hand her the papers. "I marked where the body was found. I need you to try to figure out the most likely place he went into the water. If we assume he went into the water right at or near eleven, and washed up an hour later, it couldn't have been that far out. Maybe another dock or something?"

"Are you seriously asking me to *math* right now?" She makes a show of cracking her knuckles then takes the papers. "Fine. I'm on it."

TEN

By THE TIME KAYLA FINISHES PINNING THE TIDE chart to my wall, it's almost eleven. Derek peeks at his phone. "We need to get going," he says. "Curfew."

I take the last of the pages from the printer and stick it to the murder board with a magnet. "Is it that late already?"

Kayla drapes an arm across my shoulders. "Time flies when you're solving murders."

I roll my eyes, and Derek chuckles. "Alright, you guys head out, I got it from here," I say, hugging Kayla goodbye.

Stepping back, I stare at the faces tacked to the board. Yearbook images of classmates, each smiling, looking like they are having the best day of their life. And one of them is most likely a cold-blooded killer. Uncapping a marker, I start scribbling under each image. The sound of my front door opening and closing makes me jump.

"Hello?" I call out. Replacing the marker I poke

my head out. "Derek? Kayla?"

In my kitchen, something rustles. Slipping across the hall, I retrieve Dad's 9mm from the small gun safe in his top drawer in a quick and silent move. I check the clip. Three shots. Dad never keeps it full, says it wears out the spring. Sliding the clip back in with a soft click, I hit the safety with my thumb and pull the slide. Two in the clip and one in the chamber.

With the gun pointed at the floor, I step into the hall, keeping my back against the far wall as I move silently through the house. My pulse is rapid, beating against my chest like it's fighting to escape. I take slow, deep breaths, my muscles tense. Reaching around the corner, I flick on the kitchen light and swing into the room, crouching, gun pointed at the intruder.

"Really?" Cole demands, holding up the empty pizza box.

I lower the gun, removing my finger from the trigger and replacing the safety in one smooth, well-practiced motion. "Sweet baby Jesus, Cole. You scared the shit out of me. I could have shot you."

Walking past me, he taps me on the side of the head with the empty box. "Not likely. Besides, you should have been expecting me. I sent a text."

Shaking my head, I turn my back on him, walking to my dad's room to replace the gun in the safe. When I come back, I say, "I had the ringer off.

Derek and Kayla were here. We were going over the case."

"Well, that was stupid. I thought you were avoiding me." He grins. "I should have known better."

I don't look at him as I brush past and into my office. Truthfully, I was avoiding him, and I'm not entirely sure why.

"So, what did you and the Scooby Squad come up with?"

Taking my place in front of the board, I shrug. "Not much. We put together a suspect list from the info off his tablet." I point to the first picture. "Trace Kerner, president of the photography club. Mac was blackmailing him. Apparently, Trace snuck a wireless camera into the girls locker room and was selling the photos to some Asian websites with very specific tastes."

"Why? It's not like Mac needed the cash, and I can't imagine Trace had much to give."

Reaching forward, I tap the next photo. "No, what Trace does have is an older brother who works as a bouncer-slash-ID checker at a trendy beach club. Mac took Ashleigh there for her birthday, even though they were both underage. I found some of the photos."

Cole frowns. "Sneaky. What's Brody doing on here?"

The next photo belongs to Brody Mitchell, captain of the lacrosse team and all-around-cool guy. We'd been lab partners in bio first semester. He was friendly, smart, and well liked by just about everyone. "Brody was the only person in the register with an outstanding debt from the gambling side. He owed almost twenty-six hundred dollars and was two months past due."

Cole whistles. "That's a decent chunk. But I don't know if I buy him as a murderer."

Though I tend to agree, I shake my head. "Motive, means, and opportunity. You'd be surprised what people are capable of given the right pressure. Which brings us to our final contestant, Linda Green. Turns out Linda was auctioning off her virginity on the web." I shudder. "So gross."

"Virginity?" Cole snorts. "Buyer beware."

I raise one eyebrow, but I let the comment go. Truthfully, I don't want to know. "Mac must have felt the same way, because he tanked the deal by glitching out the website. Anyone trying to bid got redirected to the FBI website."

"And of course, Cody," he says, moving to the last picture.

"Except Cody was at the dance with Ashleigh, remember? He drove her home when the dance ended at midnight."

Cole's mouth twitches. "And that's it? No other possible motives?"

"Not that I can find. Turns out that Mac shut down the gambling site a few weeks ago. Everyone was square except Brody. No one had any clue about him and Ashleigh; she didn't even tell her best friend. And of the people Mac blackmailed and or otherwise pissed off, the only three not at the dance were Trace, Brody, and Linda."

He steps back, leaning against my desk. "I don't think you can discount the people at the dance. He was last seen at the dance, after all. Did you ever figure out how he got there?"

I nod. "A couple of people saw him show up. Apparently, he walked. It's less than a mile from his house to the school."

He points to the tide charts. "And what's all this?"

There is a big section circled and colored in with red marker. "This is the most likely place he went into the water, according to the tides that night."

"That's nowhere near the dock," he says, leaning forward. "Did he swim out, and then drown? That's still a pretty long way from shore."

"But," I point at the corner of the map, "it's pretty close to the marina."

"So you're looking for a boat."

"Or someone with access to a boat, yes."

"Does Cody's family have a boat?"

I shake my head. "Nope. But both Trace and Linda's families do."

"Not Brody?"

Stepping forward, I stare at Brody's photo. "Not that I can find, but I'm not ruling him out. Not yet."

After a few moments, Cole stands, taking the red marker and adding another name to the board. *Cody Philips.* I look at him in curiosity. "It's a gut feeling." Recapping the marker, he holds it out to me. "For what it's worth," he continues, "I think you're going about this all wrong."

Folding my arms across my chest, I turn to face him as he drops into my desk chair. "Please, do tell."

"Well, there is a witness, or at least someone who knows something about what happened, and whoever it is, they really want you to figure it out."

I narrow my eyes. He's right. Maybe I have been going about this all wrong. "You're saying I should be focusing on finding the witness instead of the killer."

He nods.

I think about it for a moment. Other than tracking down my three suspect's whereabouts for the night of the murder—which I can still do anyway—there's not much else to be done now. While I roll ideas around in my head, he starts plowing through the files.

"I see you've been busy hacking the medical examiner's computer."

Turning my back to him, I sigh. "It's not hacking." I can actually feel him smirking behind my back. "Fine, it's hacking. But it's for a good cause."

"Never said it wasn't," he mumbles. "I'm just glad to see you embracing the label."

Now, I turn back to him. "I hate labels, especially that one."

"Why?" he asks, closing the folder and sitting back. "Why do you hate it so much?"

"Because, most hackers fall into two groups. They are either egotists who cause chaos because they can, or to earn some kind of notoriety, or they are activists, hacking the world in order to force some kind of political agenda. Neither are groups I want to be associated with," I say, taking a deep breath.

Cole raises his hands. "Hey, I get that. I'm sorry."

I nod curtly, taking the files from him and stacking them on the corner of my desk.

"So, bedtime?" he asks, standing. "My bag is in the car."

I freeze at his words. "I think you should go home tonight," I say, not meeting his eye as I round the desk and head into the hallway. He strides out after me.

"Are you sure? I don't want you to be alone. I can—"

I cut him off. "I'm fine, really. But you and your mom are finally making progress. Besides, I don't think Courtney appreciates you sleeping over, even if it is with good intent."

He catches my arm, turning me toward him. It's everything I have to meet his gaze without wavering. "Are you *sure*?"

I nod once. "I'm a big girl, Cole. You don't have to keep babysitting me."

"Is this because of Courtney?"

"No. I'm just tired." Gently pulling my arm free, I walk to the door, holding it open for him. "I'll see you tomorrow."

He frowns but walks out. I don't watch him. I just close the door, locking it behind him. As soon as he's out of the room, I press my back against the door. Is it about Courtney? Maybe a little. But mostly, mostly it's about me. Pulling my cell from my pocket, I scan Cole's texts before deleting them.

I'll be there after my shift.

Then...

On my way.

Once the screen is clear, I open a new message, this one to Kayla. I type it out quickly, hesitating with my thumbs over the screen.

I'm in love with Cole. I hit send and wait. It feels awful to admit it, even just in a text. It feels stupid and wrong.

Her reply comes quickly. *I know. Sorry, sweetie.*

I type again. *Yeah, me too.*

Slipping my phone back in my pocket, I push myself off the door. The house is deathly quiet as I go to my room, pulling a box from under my bed. Digging through the old scrap components, I find what I'm looking for. An old iPod Touch. Sliding the box back, I head for my office, get my toolkit from the desk drawer, and settle in.

THE NEXT MORNING COMES TOO EARLY. I CONSIDER skipping, only to remember I have a test in Physics. Reluctantly dressing, I finish tinkering with my new project while wolfing down a bowl of Lucky Charms before heading off to school.

It's a gray, dull morning, the air thick with the promise of rain. Derek and Kayla show up in her used sedan and swing into the parking spot beside me. Kayla says nothing about my late-night text, but offers me a soft pat on the back, her expression sympathetic. I spend the day trying to keep my face from betraying the level of crap-tastic I feel. At lunch, Cole slides into a seat beside me, Courtney practically attached to his hip. He offers me a cup of coffee, which I accept with a forced smile. They talk and I nod politely, giving an unenthusiastic murmur of agreement when prompted.

"You ok?" Cole asks, nudging me.

I nod, taking a long gulp of coffee, scalding my tongue. "I'm tired. Didn't sleep much last night." And it's the truth. Between being up until nearly three am, finishing up my wireless camera, and the nightmares that plagued what little sleep I did manage to get, I think I got maybe a half hour of shut eye. "I was working on something that might help me find my secret admirer."

"Secret admirer?" Courtney chimes in, her voice friendly, as if she didn't stand in this very room and call me out not a week ago. "That's romantic. Any ideas who it might be?"

Looking down at my tray, I shake my head. I'm half waiting for Cole to explain what I'm talking about, but he doesn't. He must sense my reluctance to bring her into the circle of trust.

"Yeah, someone has been leaving notes on her car," he says, leaning over so she's blocked from my line of sight.

"Well, it's nice to know romance is still alive. Some guys think bringing you cold pizza is romantic," she says, nudging Cole playfully. "What's so hard about flowers and poetry? Am I right?"

The feeling of impending vomit rolls through me.

Cole chuckles. "Farris isn't a flowers and poetry kind of girl."

I feel myself stiffen at his words. "Every girl wants romance," I say, my tone challenging. "Every girl wants to feel special. Maybe it's not candy and roses, but every girl wants romance."

He looks at me as if I have completely lost my mind.

"You see?" Courtney holds out her hand. "She knows."

"You? You want poetry?" he asks, raising one eyebrow.

I feel my hands clutching the sides of my lunch tray so hard that my knuckles go white. What can I say? That I want someone who brings me cold pizza, watches kung-fu movies with me, and who makes me soup when I'm sick? Because if I say any of that, Cole will know exactly who I'm talking about.

"No. I want Lloyd Dobbler standing outside my window with a boom box over his head playing "In Your Eyes" by Peter Gabriel." I hesitate. "Really, I just want to be with someone who gets me. And maybe I had that, and maybe I was too stupid to hold on to it."

With that, I stand, tray in hand. "I've got a test to study for. See you later."

Dropping the tray in the return bin, I burst into the hall, barely holding myself together. My hands shake so hard I have to stuff them in my pockets as I make my way to the library and what I hope will be a little peace and quiet.

The physics test turns out to be easier than I thought. I expected it to be little more than a rehash of the notes from the week prior. We are getting toward the end of the year and the teachers aren't too worried about challenging us. Most of us already have our grades for the year; this is just busy work. What I don't expect is for Courtney to corner me at my locker afterward.

"Hey," she says meekly, tucking her long, red hair back over her ear.

"Hey," I say, rooting around in my locker.

"I'm sorry about lunch," she says. "I didn't know about you and Ollie breaking up. Cole just told me." I stare at her for a full second, blinking. Cole thought I'd meant Ollie. Of course he had. How could he possibly know I'd been kicking myself for not making a move on him when I had the chance?

"Um, yeah. It's no big deal. I guess I'm just..." I trail off, not knowing quite what to say.

Reaching forward, she pulls me into a hug, and I'm so surprised that I let her. "I know. I've had my heart broken before too. I just wanted you to know that I'm sorry about that, and about what I said to you the other day. I was upset and I took it out on you. I shouldn't have. You clearly mean a lot to Cole, and I was just feeling jealous."

I force a grin. "Yeah. No hard feelings."

"Good," she says with a beaming smile. "So, some of us are having a party Friday night over on Mare Island. There's going to be a bonfire and a keg..." She trails off, excitedly twisting her body back and forth. "Cole and I are going. We want you to come. It'd mean a lot to us."

Oh God. She's using the WE. The US. The vomity feeling returns. I search her face, her posture, for any sign that she's doing it on purpose to torture me, to rub their couplehood in my face. But there's nothing. She's genuinely being nice.

It makes me want to punch her in the face.

"Sure, that sounds..." *Terrible. Awful.* Like the

worst idea on the planet. "Fun," I decide finally. Just like that, there is an unspoken truce between us. She loves Cole. I love Cole. We both want him to be happy. That means getting along, maybe even trying to be friends.

"Great. The boat leaves at eight sharp."

I force a smile. "I'll be there."

As soon as she leaves, Kayla comes up in her place. "Want me to put a hit out on her?"

I sigh, watching as Courtney and her tight blue dress sashays down the hall. "Nah. It's... fine."

She looks at me, her expression flat. "You are so full of shit."

I nod. "Pretty much. Any chance you and Derek can come keep me from going homicidal on her Friday?"

She frowns, her black lipstick and pale white face making her look like a mime from a black-and-white movie. "No can do. Derek is taking me to Charlotte for the weekend. We're going to a Deadmau5 concert. Sorry."

"Just my luck," I mutter. "On the bright side, there's always a chance I'll get hit by a bus or something between now and then."

She puts a hand on my shoulder. "Know that I love you enough to hobble you, if necessary."

"Awww, you're such a good friend."

She nods. "I know, right? Jokes aside, if you really need me to, I'll stay. Or you can bug out and go with us."

And in either scenario, I'm the third wheel. I weigh the options. At least the party will have booze if it gets too much to deal with.

"No, it's fine, really. I can do this."

The sound of Courtney's laughter floats down the hall, unmistakable. It's all I have not to turn toward the sound. "Is it bad?" I ask, closing one eye.

Kayla glances over my shoulder. "Oh yeah, you don't want to see this."

Reaching forward, she scoops me up by the arm and walks me to my car. Derek is waiting for us, leaning against Kayla's driver's side door. Releasing me, Kayla rushes to him and he lifts her off her feet, kissing her neck before releasing her. I wave to them and get in my car. Opening my bag, I retrieve my tablet and pull the mini SD card from the tiny camera on my dash. Plugging it into the tablet, I open the file. I have the camera on a motion-activated ten second burst. But all I have are a few seagulls and a leaf blowing across the hood. Swearing, I close it up. Maybe next time.

Instead of driving home, I head for the marina, the timer on my phone clocking me.

When I pull up outside the marina, I hit the stop button. Thirty-nine minutes from the school to the marina, in light traffic. The instant I open my door, the scent assaults me, salt and sand and something I can't quite place that is utterly ocean. The marina isn't gated and there's no guard. People can come and go as they please. I step on the wooden dock, and it bobs gently in the swell. Pulling out my phone, I open the note where I'd listed the names of the boats belonging to my suspect's families. First up is Linda's father's boat, the Muddy Buddy. It's a smallish fishing boat that looks like it hasn't gone anywhere in ages. Making my way further down the slips, I find the next boat on my list. The Shelby. It's huge, easily forty feet, a sleek-looking sailboat. I don't have much experience, but something tells me that it would be damn hard to take it out with just one person. It's the sort of boat that needs a crew. My phone vibrates in my hand, a text from Cole.

You home?

I reply. *Out chasing down a lead.*

It vibrates again. *You need a hand?*

I shake my head, walking back through the slips toward the parking lot beyond. *Nope. I got this.*

Sorry about today.

I bite my lip, stopping in my tracks. *No, it's my fault. I was just tired and cranky.*

Ok. Call if you need me.

I snort and slip the phone back in my jeans. Before I even reach my car door, it rings and I'm sure it's Cole, but then I see the number on the caller ID. Blocked.

"Hello?" I answer.

"Hey kiddo!"

I feel myself relax at the sound of my dad's voice. "Dad, how's life at club Med?"

"Not bad. We got to go into the city Sunday, picked you up a souvenir."

Leaning against my car, I chuckle. "A brass hookah? You know how I've always wanted one," I joke.

"Nothing so mundane." There's a rustle behind him. "Hey, it looks like I'll be seeing you soon. Some stuff got moved around, and it looks like our time will be up a little sooner than expected."

"That's awesome," I say, chewing on my bottom lip. I want to ask for dates and times, but I know better. They don't tell anyone, not even us. Wouldn't want that kind of info falling into the wrong hands. "I miss you," I blurt, sounding more desperate than I intend.

"Everything ok, kiddo?"

I sigh. "Yeah. Ollie and I broke up, that's all."

A pause, and then, "I'm sorry to hear that."

His discomfort at boy talk makes me grin. "I just miss you. I'll be glad when you're home."

"Me too, kiddo. Look, I gotta run. Someone else needs the sat phone."

"Ok, be safe, Dad."

"You too, kiddo. Love you."

"You too."

And just like that, static fills the line a moment before my cell drops the call. It's odd, how the grief comes and goes. Sometimes, I can push it out of my head, just keep putting one foot in front of the other, but then I hear his voice and I realize just how much I miss him. It hits me like being struck by lightning. Getting in the car, I drive toward home. I don't realize I'm being followed until I pull into my driveway.

ELEVEN

"**W**HAT ARE YOU DOING HERE, COLE?"

He closes his car door and jogs up to meet me on the porch. "Just checking in."

I unlock my door and push it open. The house is dark, so I flick on the lights as I move through each room, ending up in the kitchen. "I'm fine, I told you. It's just been a long couple of days. I'm just going to take a shower and go to bed."

He folds his arms across his chest. "Courtney told me she invited you to the party and you said you'd come."

Opening the fridge, I grab a bottle of water and twist open the cap. "Yep," I say, taking a drink.

"You hate parties. You hate *people*. Why did you agree to go?"

"Well, I can't keep cooped up in this house with no one to talk to but you," I say, brushing past him. "Maybe it's time for me to start getting out into the world again. I used to be fun, you know. I used to have friends."

"You have friends," he says indignantly.

I turn, glaring. "If you don't want me to go, just say so. Shit, I thought the invite came from both of you."

"It did. I do. I mean," he fumbles, "I just don't understand. Last night, you practically kicked me out, and then you barely said two words to me at school. Are you mad at me?"

He looks so genuinely confused that I actually feel bad for him. I lower the water, replacing the cap. "No, Cole, I'm not mad at anybody. I'm just, I can't keep going like this. I can't keep leaning on you like I have been. It's not healthy. You're my best friend, and I don't want to lose that, but we have to have some boundaries."

He lowers his chin. "Kayla is your friend. Do you have boundaries with her?"

I bite the inside of my cheeks. No, I don't have boundaries with Kayla. But I also don't get the urge to make out with her, either. "It's different, and you know it," I say softly.

He frowns. "Well, it was nice to be needed, even if it was just for a while."

With that, he turns and walks out the door, slamming it behind him. Part of me wants to run after him, but the other part knows it's for the best.

After my shower, I change into a tank top and shorts for bed. After tossing and turning for what feels like forever, I sit up, throwing the covers off.

Padding through the house, I step, barefoot, out the back door and into the damp grass. The moon hangs nearly full overhead, the stars shimmering in the black sky. I walk out to the old swing set. Whoever had the house before us had put it in, and we had yet to remove it. Truthfully, I kind of like it. It's simple, a metal slide and two long, chained swings. Grasping the chains in each hand, I step onto the seat and, standing upright, I swing, closing my eyes as the breeze rushes across my skin, giving the illusion of flying.

Suddenly, I'm frozen, a pair of strong hands holding me by the hips. I open my eyes, though I don't really need to. I'd know that touch anywhere.

"Cole," I say, exhaling the word.

Releasing my hips, he circles around, stepping in front of me. Taking the chains, he hoists himself onto the swing, his feet beside mine, our bodies pressed together up the length of us. I look up and his eyes shine, his face almost touching mine. He leans back and I move with him, as if we are connected, our feet swinging out from under us, then I lean back, repeating the process with him, almost lying on top of me. We swing like that, my breathing growing ragged with each movement. Every inch of me tingles, and it's a miracle I don't lose my grip. Finally, we stop moving. His hands slip down the chains, covering mine. The distance between us is so small I can feel the warmth radiating from his skin. Suddenly, I'm freezing, goose bumps breaking out across my skin. I'm the moth, and he's the flame. I'm drowning, and he's dry land.

He whispers my name, lowering his lips to mine.

Closing my eyes, I wait, desperate to feel his mouth, the warmth of his hands on my skin.

My alarm goes off and I slam upright in bed, the last flickering remnants of the dream shattering like glass. I look at my phone. Three messages from Cole.

I delete them without reading them.

Clearly, Cole is a drug and I need to detox.

THE WEEK FLIES BY WITHOUT A PEEP FROM MY mysterious tipster. In the meantime, Brody and Linda have alibied out of the suspect pool. Brody was on a plane on the way to visit family in Nashville, and Linda was in the hospital with the stomach flu. That left Trace and Cody, their photos staring at me from the murder board.

I should be getting ready for tonight's festivities—what does one wear to a drunken beach party?—but I'm procrastinating. Truth is, I've been hiding since Ollie left town, and it is far past time to quit. I need to get up, get out, and get over it. Steeling myself, I go to my bedroom, keeping on my well-worn blue jeans and picking a slightly nicer shirt, a black cami with lace along the bottom, and add a rhinestone-studded bar necklace. I take my hair out of the carefully plaited braid and shake it free, my brown hair falling into loose waves past my shoulders.

Beach party casual.

Taking my wallet out of my bag, I attach the chain to my front belt loop and tuck it in my back pocket. Slipping my phone in my front jean pocket, I grab a black-and-blue plaid flannel shirt as I head for the car.

The marina buzzes with people when I pull in. Kids from school in shorts and flip-flops carry coolers down the wooden deck and toward the small boat ferrying people over to the island. As soon as she sees me, Courtney rushes over, pulling me into a hug.

"You made it," she says, giggling. "I told you she'd come."

Cole steps up beside her. "You were right." He turns to me. "I'm glad you're here."

I smile. Truth is, I'd managed to avoid him almost all week. Other than the occasional check-in text, he'd kept his space. It was a mixed blessing, really. "Yeah, wouldn't miss it," I say, trying to sound cheerful.

Another group of people arrives behind me. Courtney quickly moves around to greet them, leaving Cole and me in awkward silence.

"So," he says finally, "you heard from your dad?"

"Yeah, he called the other day. Seems to be doing

good. He says they might get home a little early."

"That'd be cool."

I nod. "How's your mom?"

He shrugs. "She's fine. Things are calmer, I think. I'm trying to be civil."

"Well, you know, that's what you have to do sometimes. You both love her, want her to be happy. So you try to play nice." I glance at Courtney, who is chatting with a brunette I don't recognize. When I look back at Cole, he's staring at me, an odd expression on his face.

He opens his mouth to say something, but I cut him off, "Look, here's our ride."

The skiff is decent sized, with a maroon bottom and white trim. Justin Malloy is at the helm, doing a quick donut before killing the motor and docking at the edge of the deck while another guy ties the boat off.

"All aboard," he announces, drawing a cheer from the crowd.

Stepping past Cole, I take Justin's hand and let him help me into the boat. Truth is, I've been dying to talk to Cody, hopefully cross him off the suspect list. But it seems impossible to ask him if he knew his girlfriend was cheating on him without spilling the beans if he didn't. So, I'd settled on chatting up his friend Justin instead. Justin doesn't have a reputation for being a ladies' man, but he certainly could be, with his shaggy, brown hair and bright blue eyes. He has a small mouth, but a really great smile. As I watch him helping people onto the skiff, I try to lock down a plan of attack.

I'll need to get him alone, away from the crowd, that much is certain. Maybe I can bond with him over the lament of being a third wheel. Yes, I think that will be the ticket.

Courtney and Cole step on last, and Cole reaches over to untie the boat from the dock.

With a clap, Justin fires up the engine and spins the boat back toward open water. I lean back, letting the breeze blow across my face and through my hair, just enjoying the sea spray on my skin. It's nearly full dark, and I know without looking that the water will be black around us, as if we are gliding through the sky instead of water. I don't open my eyes until I feel the boat slow, throttling back as we approach the beach. There's no dock here, so he lets the boat drift until the flat bottom brushes the shore. Dropping the anchor, he hops off, the water only a few inches deep, and begins offering hands again. When he reaches out to me, I smile, pretending to slip just a little so he has to half catch me.

Smiling politely, he finishes helping me onto dry sand.

"Thanks," I mutter, looking up at him from under my lashes, as if embarrassed.

He blinks, as if seeing me for the first time. "My pleasure."

And with that, I follow the line of people heading across the center of the island, through the path cut in the tall grass that leads to the other side. The path is lit with dozens of small, solar lights poking out of the sand, creating an otherworldly glow.

I see the flames before I even break through the grass. The entire beach is illuminated in flickers of red and orange. There are four huge driftwood logs circling the fire. Beyond that, blankets and towels are spread out everywhere. Some people are sitting on the logs, some on the blankets. Some are just standing around, red Solo cups in hand as they chat. There's a small group of guys in lawn chairs playing acoustic guitars and beating on a set of bongos. One of them is plucking at a ukulele while he sings softly.

The keg is set up on a pallet and a small line has formed. I'm not much of a drinker anyway, but I tend to be especially careful at parties where I hardly know anyone, but I also know the value of blending in. I'm about to walk over when someone hands me a cup. I recognize him immediately. Scott Stewart, one of Oliver's old friends and the football team place kicker.

"You look like you could use this," he says, his tone friendly.

"You have no idea," I say, lifting the cup to my mouth and pretending to take a drink.

Scott is tall, over six feet if I had to guess, and thinner than most of the other guys on the team.

He has sandy-brown hair, light green eyes, and a dimple in the tip of his nose.

"I haven't seen you around for a while," he says, waving to someone as they pass behind me. "How's life treating you?"

I almost laugh. "It's been a little crazy, to be honest. How about you?"

He shakes his head. "Can't complain. I managed to land a scholarship to Georgia Tech."

"Wow, hey, that's awesome. Congrats."

"Thanks."

We continue chatting pleasantly for a few more minutes before he excuses himself to go join in on a game of beach checkers. As soon as I turn around, I see Ashleigh making a beeline for me and I swear under my breath.

"Farris, there's someone I want you to meet," she says, taking me by the arm without waiting for a response. She drags me across the beach and taps a familiar boy on the shoulder. He turns, and I'm face to face with Brody Mitchell.

"Brody, this is Farris, the girl I was telling you about," she says, beaming.

"Right, we had bio together first quarter. Nice to see you again," he says, holding out a hand for me to shake.

"Yeah, how's it going?" I ask pleasantly.

He makes a face. "Been better. Did you see the game last week?"

Lacrosse, right. "No, I missed it. But I heard it was a hell of a game."

He snorts. "We got our asses handed to us. Again. But hey, you can't win them all, right?"

"That's what I hear," I offer, watching out the corner of my eye as Cole leans over Courtney's shoulder and whispers something in her ear. From her expression, it isn't something pleasant.

"What about you? I haven't seen you outside of school in a while."

God, I'm a hermit. People think I'm a hermit.

"Yeah, you know, I've been busy. Truthfully, I'm a bit of a homebody. Crowds like this are not really my thing." I raise my cup. "But I'm trying to get out more."

"Well, you picked a good party to make your grand reentrance. Normally, the freshmen crash the parties and things just get out of hand. Justin did a good job keeping this just for the upperclassmen. Very calm, just the cool people."

Looking around, I see that he's right. It's not a huge crowd. No one is loud, crazy, or stumbling drunk. It's very mellow, considering. "Yeah, it's really nice."

"Cheers," he says, holding his cup out.

I tap it with my own and fake taking another drink. "That reminds me... I wanted to go thank Justin for the invite. I'll talk to you later?" I say, scanning the crowd.

"I'll be around," Brody says with a grin, turning back to his group of friends.

When I finally lock eyes on Justin, he's sitting on one of the logs, gently swaying to the cover being played. Walking over, I look down at him. "Hey, this seat taken?" I ask.

He smiles and waves for me to have at it.

"So," I begin, "I wanted to thank you for the invite. I get the feeling this is by special invitation only. I don't get many invites anymore."

He swishes his cup of beer around. "No problem. I'm glad you could come."

"Me too. It's nice to get out again." I pause. "Although honestly, I was kind of afraid I'd end up being the third wheel again." I nod to where Cole and Courtney are standing in the distance, deep in conversation.

Beside me, Justin takes a long drink. I follow his gaze across the fire to where Ashleigh sits on Cody's lap. "Yeah, I get that."

"You too, huh?"

He nods. "Hey, sorry to hear about you and Ollie. He was a good guy."

I can't help the look of surprise that comes over my face. "How did you know?"

He snickers. "Courtney has a big mouth."

I roll my eyes. Of course she does. Then it dawns on me. "Oh God, I think she's trying to set me up with Brody." I feel the irritation brewing inside me.

"That's why she invited me." Staring down at my cup, I wonder how I could have been so stupid.

"Well, you know what they say, the best revenge is having a good time," he offers.

I look at him in suspicion. "Do they really say that?"

He shrugs. "I don't know, but they should."

To hell with it, I decide, holding up my cup. "To having fun then." This time when I raise my cup, I don't pretend to drink.

Standing, Justin walks over to the guitar players, says something, then takes one and sits down. He waves me over and I obey, taking a seat on the log facing them.

"This song is dedicated to Farris," he says in a loud voice, drawing the attention of the people nearby, and then they start playing.

I feel my face blush.

"Well, shake it up baby, now," Justin sings. "Twist and shout."

Immediately, everyone begins to flock to the music and sing along. I clap, unable to keep the embarrassed smile off my face. Soon, I'm on my feet, dancing away. It feels good—liberating. I don't remember the last time I danced like this. By the time he reaches the end of the song, everyone is clapping, dancing, and singing. He hits the last chord, and the crowd bursts into applause.

Standing, he bows, then slips his hand around

my waist and swings me into a dip. He lowers his head like he's kissing me, but he just presses his cheek to mine and whispers, "Third wheels unite."

I laugh, and I'm still laughing when he swings me back onto my feet.

The music picks up again, and the crowd, now having caught the fever, dances again. I let Justin lead me away, toward the keg for a refill.

"Where did you learn to play like that?" I ask, holding my cup with my teeth as I tug down my shirt that had ridden up during his enthusiastic dip.

"Theater camp, middle school," he says, making a dramatic hand gesture. I hand him my cup and he fills it, then hands it back to me.

"Ok, I gotta ask. Why are you still single?" I say as we continue down the beach until the surf is lapping at my feet. The party rages on behind us, but we are far enough away that the music is faint.

He half laughs, and not in a jovial way. "Same as you, I guess. If you can't be with the one you love..."

Then I remember the glance he'd given Ashleigh and Cody. Of course. He's in love with Ashleigh too. I decide to finish his sentence for him. "Then pine away hopelessly from a distance?"

"Exactly."

"Didn't realize it was that obvious," I admit.

He shrugs. "Like recognizes like, I guess. Though, for what it's worth, I think he's into you too. If he weren't, Courtney wouldn't be trying to set you up with someone else. She's worried about you. And she should be."

"No, she really shouldn't," I say flatly. "I'm not the kind of girl to make a move on someone else's boyfriend."

He gives me a side glance. "That's kind of refreshing actually. Not many people have a moral compass when it comes to wanting someone."

I bite at my bottom lip. "That sounds like experience talking. So, who burned you?"

He shakes his head. "It's a long, depressing story."

I take another drink from my cup, and he does the same. "Well, I've got nowhere to be," I offer.

He pauses, opening his mouth to say something, but before he can get a word out, Cole jogs up to us. "Hey, great song, man."

"Thanks," Justin says, offering me a pointed look. "Well, looks like I need a refill. Catch you later, Farris."

He jogs off, and I slug Cole in the arm.

"Idiot. I was this close to getting him to spill the beans on Cody and Ashleigh." I hold up my thumb and forefinger, almost touching them together.

Cole raises his hands. "Sorry. I just wanted to make sure you were ok after he practically molested you back there."

"He did not almost molest me, my God." I pause. "And did you know that Courtney only invited me to try to hook me up with Brody?"

Now he looks sufficiently embarrassed. "I didn't know until we got here. I'm really sorry about that. I told her to knock it off."

Turning my back to him, I face out at the ocean. The breeze blows across the surface of the water and chills me. Maybe it's because I'm flushed from the beer or the dancing, but goose bumps erupt across my bare arms. And of course, I forgot my flannel in the car.

"Here," Cole says, slipping out of his dark blue zip hoodie. "Take this."

He moves to drape it across my shoulders, but I flinch away. "Have you lost your damn mind?" I ask. "You don't put your jacket on another girl when your girlfriend is twenty feet away staring at you."

He looks over his shoulder and then back at me. "You looked cold."

"I am cold. But I don't need you to fix it, Cole. Don't you see that it upsets her?"

He sighs. "Sometimes, I feel like I can never do the right thing with you."

I shake my head. "I don't get it. Honestly. If you care about Courtney, and you know it upsets her that we're close, then why do you do it? Either you love her or you don't."

"You don't get it because you aren't like her. Courtney, she's easy."

I raise one eyebrow.

"No." He holds out his hands. "Not like that. I mean girls like Courtney are easy to be with. I know what she wants, and I know how to make her happy. She's very... basic."

"You know that's not a compliment, right?"

Frustrated, he runs his fingers through his hair. "This isn't coming out right. What I'm trying to say is, girls like you are... dangerous. Girls who know who they are and what they want, girls who understand their value and won't accept less than they're worth. Girls like that are hurricanes—easy to get caught up in and capable of wreaking real havoc. Girls like you are forces of nature." He pauses, realizing what he's just said. "Guys like me live in fear of disappointing girls like you."

"And girls like Courtney are, what?"

"Girls like Courtney, yeah, they might get pissed. But I take her flowers, tell her she's pretty, and all is forgiven. She is never going to hold me to a standard I can't live up to. She's never going to look at me the way you're looking at me right now."

I look away at the accusation in his voice. "That is..." I hesitate, taking a deep breath and raising my chin, "such total horse shit. You shouldn't be with someone because they're easy not to disappoint. You should be with someone because they challenge you. Because you feel more like yourself when you're with them. Because the thought of not having them in your life makes you feel like the air's been sucked out of the room. Love isn't *easy*. It's scary as hell. It turns you upside down and inside out and makes you beg for just one more ride."

"You know, people in glass houses shouldn't throw stones, Farris. Maybe I'm not in the mood to take relationship advice from the girl who just broke my best friend's heart," he says, folding his arms across his chest.

His words are daggers, slicing through me. I step back, the anger rushing out like the tide, only to be replaced with crashing waves of guilt.

"Farris..." He reaches out, but I hold up my hands.

"No, you're right. I'm gonna go. Have a nice time with your girlfriend," I say, walking down the beach, back toward the glowing path. As I pass the keg, I see Justin standing there, chatting.

"Hey Justin, I hate to do it, but could you give me lift back to the marina?"

He nods, handing off his cup. "Sure. No problem."

We walk side by side away from the sounds of the party and the flickering light of the bonfire. "Did that look as bad as it was?" I ask as I step into the boat.

Justin pushes it off the shore as I bring up the anchor. "Not really. What did he say?"

I press my lips together, making a sour face before answering. "He said that he's with Courtney because she's less complicated than other girls. He doesn't have to try as hard with her."

"Do you think that's true? That some people

are easier to love than others?" he asks seriously, bringing the motor sputtering to life.

"Yeah, I guess that's true," I say finally, half shouting over the engine noise. After all, falling for Oliver had been easy. He was far from uncomplicated, but being with him had been simple. Easy.

Maybe that's why it didn't last.

"Then you can't really fault him for feeling that way. Maybe he just needs something a little simple in his life right now. And face it, just because you can handle something harder, it doesn't mean he can."

Staring at him, I realize two things. First off, that's he's right and I've been a total ass. Secondly, that he's been exactly in my shoes, in love with someone who would be a messy, complicated relationship.

He's in love with Ashleigh, too.

And that makes him a suspect.

The ride back to the marina is quiet after that, but when he helps me off the boat, I hug him. I hug him because he sang for me. Because he'd taken me out of there when I'd asked, no question. But mostly, I hug him because he understood and maybe, just maybe, that was worth something.

When I get to my car, I notice a piece of white paper stuck under my wiper. Taking it off carefully, I open it and read the message.

Having fun partying with a murderer?

TWELVE

Sliding into the car, I pull the mini camera off the dash and remove the SD card. I don't have my tablet, so I won't know until I get home if I got a decent picture of the witness, but the thought is enough to distract me from my emotional turmoil.

The drive home is slow. I didn't drink enough to get a buzz, and the boat ride over cleared my head of what little fog there was, but I am extra cautious anyway. I turn off the radio, roll the windows down, and just let the wind whip through the car. As soon as I pull into the driveway, I know what I want to say.

Pulling out my phone, I send a text to Cole. *Sorry I was a dick.* As I walk to the door, the response comes.

Ditto. We good?

I reply. *We good. Bring coffee in the morning and I will fill you in.*

He texts back. *Sure thing, bossy pants. See you in the am.*

Pushing the front door open, I realize that

something is wrong. It's not something I hear or see. It's a feeling, a wrongness that I can't quite place. Flicking the lights on as I go, I carefully examine each room. The house is empty, silent. When I get to my office, I push open the door and a strange odor hits me. It's faint, but distinct. Men's cologne. I scour the room, not sure what I'm looking for. Hidden cameras, microphones, anything at all. Everything seems untouched. Maybe it was just my imagination, exhaustion mixed with alcohol. Paranoia at its finest.

Booting up the computer, I run a full scan, looking for any hidden malware or spyware. While that's running, I get the tablet out of my backpack and plug in the SD card. I scroll through a dozen or so images before I see it. A hand leaving a note. Three dark, blurry shots later, I have a decent snap. I have to run it through a few clean-up filters but finally, a decent image fills the screen. I've seen her around school, but she's a senior and I'm not even sure what her name is. But I know she's on the swim team. Quickly pulling up last year's yearbook online, I scan over the pages until I hit the swim team. There she is, smiling in black and white.

Cho Pierce.

As soon as my computer scan comes back clean, I start accessing her social media accounts. Cho is a top-notch swimmer, state champ two years running, the senior class secretary, and all-around overachiever. Her family's pretty middle class. Mother is Chinese-American, her father an AIMD Sergeant from Kentucky. She has two brothers, twins, both in middle school. She doesn't have a boyfriend, but she seems to be well liked by most of her teammates. And as far as I can find, she has no connection at all to Mac, Ashleigh, or the gambling site.

So how the hell does she fit in to all this?

Printing out her photo, along with a picture of Justin, I tack them to the murder board. Then, unable to shake the strange feeling in my gut, I pack a bag and close up the house, driving to the only place I can think to go.

Cole's mom answers the door. "Farris, is everything ok?" she asks, ushering me inside. "Cole's out tonight; I'm not sure when he'll be back."

I wince. "I know, and I'm sorry to do this, but can I crash on your couch tonight? My house is just a little, I don't know. I got kind of freaked out being all alone, I guess."

She pulls me into a tight hug. Cole's mom is about the only person on the planet whose hugs I enjoy. "Of course, dear." She motions to the living room. "You go make yourself comfortable. I'll get a pillow and some blankets."

"Thanks," I say, hoping she can hear the gratitude in my voice. Pulling some pajamas out of my bag, I change quickly in the guest bathroom. By the time I come back, she has the couch all made up for me. "Here you go sweetheart," she says. This time, I initiate the hug. "Sweet dreams, Farris."

"You too," I say, nestling in. The lack of sleep overwhelms me and before I know it, I'm fading out. The last thought in my head is that the pillow smells like Cole.

THE SCENT OF COFFEE WAKES ME. I BLINK AND SEE Cole sitting on the floor across from me, two mugs in hand. I sit up suddenly. "I'm sorry. I meant to text you that I was coming over."

He hands me a mug. "Relax, its fine. Mom said you got freaked out last night?"

I shake my head. "Not exactly, but the truth makes me sound crazy, so..."

Pushing the blankets aside, he sits next to me. "What happened? Did Justin hurt you?"

I take a sip, flinching at the burn on my tongue. "No. No, nothing like that. It's just, I got home and... ok, this sounds nuts, but I think someone was in my house. Like, I smelled someone."

"Someone was in your house?"

"No, I mean they were gone when I got there, but I smelled cologne in my office."

He leans back. "Are you sure?"

I frown. "Yes. No. I mean, it was late and I was

tired. It's possible I was imagining it. But there was no way I was gonna be able to stay there. So I came here and your mom gave me the couch. I meant to text you."

"Are you okay?" he asks, wrapping one arm around me.

It's only then that I realize I'm trembling, my voice high and closing in on hysteria. *Come on, Farris. Get a grip.* "I'm fine now. To be honest, I haven't slept that well in a week."

"Are you okay to go back to your house? I want to have a look around." His blue eyes are intense, his expression serious.

I nod. "Yeah. I'm fine. It was just a weird feeling. Probably nothing."

He squeezes me once before releasing me to stand. "Well, let's have some coffee, then you can put some clothes on and we will go check things out."

I nod, taking a sip. "Oh, and for the record, I always need you. Even when I'm being a judgmental bitch."

"Noted."

"Now, for God's sake, go put a shirt on. Who do you think you are, Magic Mike?"

He snickers and starts dancing around. "I wasn't the one shaking it at the beach last night."

"What was I supposed to do? He was playing my jam." I grin over the top of my cup. "I've never been serenaded before. Apparently, it's a real panty dropper."

He stops in mid-move and scowls. "Justin? For real? Are you into him?"

I frown. "Nope. Actually, I think he might be a murderer. Such a waste."

"And you went off into the dark with him anyway?"

Offering him a flat look, I wave my hand, "Give me a little credit. I was pumping him for info. Speaking of, I found out who my mystery tipster is. She left another note last night."

"She?"

I nod. "Now get dressed and we can go play with the murder board."

He shrugs, flipping his hair playfully, and heads back to his room. I drain the last of my still-too-warm coffee and head for the bathroom to toss on a fresh pair of jeans and my olive-green tank top. Over that, I add the flannel I'd forgotten in the car the night before and a necklace with a hidden flash drive inside. Pulling my hair into a high ponytail, I slide my feet into my baby-blue Converse low tops and go back to the living room, folding up my blankets.

Cole reappears in a pair of black jeans and a gray T-shirt. "Need any help?" he asks as I fold up the last blanket.

"Nah. I'm done. Is your mom around? I want to thank her again."

He shakes his head. "She had an early meeting and won't be back till after lunch."

Grabbing my bag, I slip it over one shoulder. "Ok then, let's go."

As we are walking out the door, his phone beeps. He looks at it quickly before tucking it back in his jeans. I want to ask if it's Courtney, if everything is all right. But I bite my tongue. After the monumental ass I'd made of myself last night, I don't feel like getting into another battle.

My house is exactly as I'd left it. The foreign smell is long evaporated. Cole takes his time, looking through every closet, cabinet, and drawer. I head straight for my office, booting up my electronics. When he finally joins me, I'm hacking away at my keyboard. He half sits on the corner of the desk, folding his arms across his chest as he examines the newest additions to the board.

"Cho Pierce, that's so random," he mutters.

"How so?" I ask, not looking up from my program.

He shrugs. "I don't know her well, but she always seemed so straight laced, you know? So if she did see something, then why not just go to the police?"

"There are lots of reasons. The biggest is usually just fear. Fear makes people flee when they should fight, run when they should help. It's a very normal reaction." I pause. "Until I talk to her, I won't know anything."

"How do you even start that conversation? Hey, I

hear you saw a murder, so let's chat about that."

I execute the program and sit back in my chair. "I'll burn that bridge when I get to it. In the meantime, I need to track her down."

"You can find her at school Monday," he suggests.

I shake my head. "No, I want to catch her somewhere quieter. I set up a program to monitor her social media accounts. The next time she posts, it'll send me a text with her location."

"You're good, you know that?"

I crack my knuckles. "Tell me something I don't know."

"So, what do we do in the meantime?"

"We're going to go see a man about a boat."

THE MARINA LOOKS DIFFERENT IN THE LIGHT OF DAY. People trod up and down the dock, taking boats out and bringing them back. I round the far corner and point to the lonely slip in front of the marina office. "That's the skiff Justin used last night. Either he rented it or stole it. It would be helpful to know which," I say, opening the door and climbing the narrow stairs to the office.

The receptionist is an older woman, her face slender and worn like leather. Too many years of sunbathing and smoking taking its toll. Beside her, a small glass ashtray houses the remains of a half dozen cigarettes. I can't help but cringe, hoping they aren't all hers and they aren't all from today. Her yellow smile suggests otherwise.

"What can I do for you?" she asks, her voice pleasant, if a bit gravely.

"I was wondering about that skiff down below. Is that something we could rent?" She eyes me suspiciously, so I continue, "We're doing a project for biology, charting the migration patterns of the local dolphin pods."

She pulls a dusty paper ledger from below the desk and slides it toward me.

"Normally, it's just for members, but I can probably make an exception, just this once. The fee is fifty dollars for an hour, and I'll need a copy of your license."

Opening my wallet, I hand over my debit card and ID. "Gotta make a copy, be sure to sign the ledger with your check out time, and then check back in when you're done."

I smile and nod. When she turns her back to make a copy, I open the ledger, scanning the names. There's nothing recorded for last night or the night of the murder. I sign my name, scrawling it as illegibly as possible.

She slides my cards back across the desk and hands over a set of keys. "One hour," she reminds us, giving Cole a sidelong glance.

"Yes, ma'am," he says, tapping on the desk with his knuckles.

We get down to the boat, and I begin untying it from the dock. "Tell me you know how to operate one of these things," I say.

Climbing on board, he takes the keys and cranks the engine. "My grandfather had a fishing boat. We used to go out every day during the summer." He hesitates, looking at the dash. "It's like riding a bike."

His tone isn't inspiring much confidence, but he manages to get us turned and away from the dock. Pulling the tide maps out of my back, I read off the coordinates.

"What's out there?" he asks, the boat buzzing across the water.

"I'm timing us. I need to know how long it takes to get to the drop zone and back," I answer, starting the timer on my phone.

The trip is short and quiet. When he finally cuts back the throttle, leaving us drifting, he turns to me. "We're here."

I hit the timer.

"That was quick, less than ten minutes. Say another five to drop the body, and then ten minutes back, that gives us half hour, give or take five minutes. Add another thirty minutes to get from the school to the marina and get the body to the skiff. Assuming the text was sent at the same time the body was dumped, that means the body went into the water right at ten forty-five. The killer could have been back at the dance by eleven forty-five.

Which means they would have to leave the dance by nine forty-five. That's about fifteen minutes after his argument with Ashleigh."

"What does that mean?"

I stare at Cole. "It means that anyone at that dance could have done it. And the person with motive and access to the boat is Justin. I just need to talk to Cho, find out what she saw and when she saw it. Maybe I can come up with something to hand over to the police."

"Do you think there's evidence on the boat?" he asks, looking around.

"Doesn't matter. The entire senior class was on this boat last night. Even if there was some kind of trace evidence, it's no good now. Too contaminated." A large boat passes us, making the skiff roll in its wake. I clutch the metal sides. "Let's get back to shore. I wanna go track down Cho."

Without further discussion, Cole turns us about and heads back to shore.

We're halfway back to base when my text alert goes off. "Cho just posted a selfie. The location tag in the image puts her at Starbucks, the one by the pool hall."

Cole nods, taking a sharp left. "Remind me never to get on your bad side."

"I thought that was a given," I say, pulling my tablet out and tossing my bag in the back seat. "And drive faster. You just got passed by a van full of nuns."

"I'm doing the speed limit," he counters, and I roll my eyes.

"At this rate, she will have already consumed her skinny vanilla chi latte and be gone," I mutter.

"You can tell what she's ordering?"

Putting the tablet down, I make a face. "No. I'm just screwing with you."

"It's a good thing you're cute," he mutters, taking a right into the parking lot.

I put my hand over my heart mockingly. "Aww, you think I'm cute?"

He parks and points to the coffee shop. "Get out."

"Wow, who's a bossy pants now?" I say, exiting the car.

Making a quick beeline for the shop, I see Cho sitting inside in a high-back red velvet chair, book in hand. The shop is nearly empty, a few people chatting at a tall corner table, the music playing gently in the background. Without preamble, I drop into the seat across from her.

"Cho, right?" I wait until she looks up at me, carefully gauging her reaction. To her credit, there's no shock, just an expression of mild boredom. "I got your message," I continue, "but I have a few questions I need answered."

She closes the book, setting it in her lap. "I'm sorry, do I know you?"

Tapping my tablet, I bring up her photo, flipping it over in my hands for her to see. "Fine. Let's pretend I'm not the smartest person in this room. Let's also assume you didn't come to me knowing I could probably unravel this mess. You really should have assumed I was at least smart enough to figure out who was leaving notes on my car."

Leaning forward, she narrows her eyes. "You can't prove anything."

I cock my head. "I don't need to prove anything, not to you. I do, however, have the pesky task of proving to the cops that Justin Malloy killed Mac. I assume you would like to see that happen?"

She sits back, nodding once.

"Good, then help a girl out. If you saw what went down, why didn't you call the police?"

Scanning the room, she leans forward again. "I didn't call the police because..." She hesitates, sizing me up.

"Look, I'm not gonna say anything. Like you said, I've got no proof you saw anything. But I need to know what went down so I can try to come up with some evidence linking Justin to the body. And I know you can help with that. I also know you must be feeling pretty damn guilty to bring me into it, so just tell me already."

"It was the night of the dance. I snuck into the coach's office to switch out the results of my drug test." Immediately, she launches into the defensive. "It wasn't even my fault! Those assholes spiked the brownies at Megan Reiley's party with pot. We have to test before state qualifiers. I knew I'd pop, so I needed to get in and switch the samples."

"Which is why you can't go to the police," I say, folding my arms across my chest. "Because you'd have to explain why you were there."

"I can't lose my scholarship. If I pop, they'd drop me, and my family can't afford to send me to college any other way. I've worked my entire life for this—"

I hold up my hand, cutting her off. "Got it. I'm not judging. Well, not much at any rate. Get to what you saw."

"I was in the office switching samples, and I heard some people come in. The coach has cameras in the pool—they don't record unless you set them, like for meets and stuff—but they're always live. So I turned on the monitor to see who was out there. I saw Mac come in; Justin and Cody must have already been inside. There's no sound, and I couldn't make what they were saying, but they started yelling and pushing each other. Mac punched Justin, and Cody jumped in. Then my cell rang, my stupid date looking for me. I was afraid they heard it, so I flipped off the monitor and hid under the desk."

"Did they find you?" I ask.

She shakes her head. "No, I don't even think they heard it. After a few minutes, I came out and turned the monitor back on to see if they were gone. I saw Justin pulling Mac's body out of the pool and dragging it out the back exit."

"Where was Cody?"

She shrugs. "Gone. I waited until they were gone and ran back to the dance. I wanted to call the cops, I swear to God I did, but Mac was already dead and I was..."

"Scared?"

She nods. "Terrified. The next day, I heard Mac killed himself, or so the paper said. I knew I couldn't let it go. I couldn't let people think he died like that. But, I couldn't come forward. Then I remembered you, and how you figured out that hacking thing last year. So I did the only thing I could. I just hoped you'd put it together without having to come forward."

I frown. "And that's all you know? Absolutely?"

She nods. I nibble on the inside of my lip. If Mac drowned in a pool, the medical examiner should have caught it. And the wound on his head—how had that happened?

"What are you going to do?"

I put my hands on my knees, preparing to stand. "I'm going to go see if I can find some evidence to prove what you saw."

"And you'll keep me out of it?"

I sigh, standing. "Yeah. It won't be the first dirty secret I've kept this week."

"Thanks," she says, her voice meek.

I wave over my shoulder and head back to the car where Cole waits.

"What, no coffee?" he asks.

"Not yet. Do you think we can get into the school on a Sunday?" I ask.

He turns over the engine. "I'm sure we can come up with something."

Sitting back, I buckle and put my boots up on the dash.

"You okay?" he asks. "You look upset."

I rub my face. "I guess I'm just tired of being disappointed by people. Is it really that hard to be a decent freaking human being?"

"Maybe you just expect too much of people," he offers. "Everyone has weaknesses, and everyone falls short sometimes. We can't all be perfect, Farris. We can't all be like you."

I snort. "If you're insinuating that I'm perfect, then you haven't been paying attention."

"Oh, God no. You're bossy and bitchy and judgmental."

"Thanks," I mutter.

"I think the difference is that most people try to hide their flaws, you just own them. You wear that shit like armor," he says, not looking at me.

Before I can decide what to say to that, my phone vibrates. "Derek and Kayla are back in town. They want to meet up for dinner later. You in?"

He flinches. "I can't. I promised Courtney I'd come over tonight."

His words surprise me, a quick flash of irritation rippling through me. I exhale, pushing it aside. It's good. He *should* be spending time with her, and I need to be supportive even if it stings like lemon juice in a paper cut.

"That's cool," I say, texting Kayla back. *Rapscallions at 6?* It's one of Derek's favorite places, mostly because he slaughtered the hot wing challenge there last summer and still has his photo on the wall.

Kayla responds quickly. *See you there.*

I tuck my phone away just as we pull into the parking lot behind the gym. We try all the doors, with no luck. Finally, we circle back to the car and he points up, to the small windows that lead into the boy's locker room. One is open just a fraction.

"You have lost your damn mind," I say, staring at the small gap.

"I won't fit. Come on, I'll hoist you up, you climb in, then come around and open the door for me." Bracing his back against the brick wall, he hunches over, locking his hands together in a small cradle.

Putting one foot in his hands, I grasp his shoulders. "Do not drop me."

He grins. "Never."

On the count of three, he stands, hoisting me into the air. I catch the window frame and lurch halfway inside, pausing to listen. There's no sound, no hint that anyone else is in the room, but the smell is so awful I gag when I take a breath. It's like the inside of a zombie's jock strap, a rotted, sour sweat smell that makes my eyes burn. Wriggling my way in, I fall forward, hitting the floor with a loud thump and a gasp as the air evacuates my lungs. For a moment, I just stay still, my shoulder and hip aching from the impact.

"That's gonna leave a mark," I mutter to no one. When I can finally climb to my feet, I hobble out of the locker room to the gym door and push it open for Cole, who stares at me expectantly. I'm holding one arm gingerly and he reaches out, cupping my elbow.

"You okay there, turbo?"

I raise my uninjured arm and flip him off.

"Well, your winning personality is intact, that's good. Come on." He leads me down the hall. "The pool is over here."

He pushes the door open and I step in, realizing I've never actually been in this room before. It's an Olympic-size pool, five feet deep on one side, going to twelve feet on the far end by the diving boards.

"Do you smell that?" I ask, brushing past him.

He shakes his head. "What?"

"Not chlorine," I say, walking to the edge and scooping up a handful of water. I take a sip and then spit it onto the concrete. "Salt water. It's a salt water pool. The medical examiner wouldn't know the difference unless he tested it, and there was no reason to. This is where Mac drowned."

"And then, what?"

I can see it in my head, playing like a movie. I see Justin pulling him out of the water, dragging him to the single door leading to the parking lot. "Justin and Cody put the body in one of their trunks, drove to the marina, took the body out a little ways, dumped him, sent the text, dumped the phone too, then came back like nothing happened."

I shake my head. "If we knew who's car they moved the body in, we could search the trunk for trace evidence. But there's no way to know which car they used."

"And I think Justin has a truck. If the body was in the back of that, he probably hosed it out already," Cole adds.

I circle the pool slowly, my eyes searching for the thing missing from the equation. "The head wound," I say. "It happened here; he went into the water unconscious. So where did the head wound come from?"

"Maybe he hit it on the floor?"

I point to the rescue hook suspended against the wall. The telescoping rod is metal and only a little longer than a baseball bat collapsed. "Or maybe they hit him with something like that?" Walking over, I examine it without touching it. "Even if they didn't hit him with it, if he drowned in the deep end, they had to fish him out somehow without getting themselves all wet, right?"

"Fingerprints?" Cole asks.

"And blood probably." I walk over to Cole. "Think about it, they didn't have time to clean up, not well anyway. So they probably just washed off everything with pool water, and since there's no chlorine in the water, there should still be some trace of blood in the concrete. We just need to find it."

"Luminol," Cole says. "It's what they use on TV when they need to find blood that you can't see with the naked eye."

"We can probably find out how to make it online," I offer. "Or just buy it outright."

He holds out his hand. "To the Batcave, Robin?"

"No, you're going to drop me off at home, and then go get ready for your date. I'll deal with the luminol." I pause. "And why do I have to be Robin?"

"Because I'm driving—that makes me Batman."

"Actually, that makes you Alfred," I point out.

He considers it for a moment. "I'll take it."

THIRTEEN

As it turns out, you can make luminol from household chemicals, if you have a week and the patience of a saint. Seeing as I have neither, I order it on Amazon and have it overnight shipped. Sitting at my desk, I rifle through Justin's social media accounts. Pictures of him with Ashleigh and Cody stare back at me, a grim reminder that one or both of these guys is a killer. And not just that, they covered it up, made it look like he killed himself. And for what? Some stupid girl who wanted to walk on the wild side?

For the life of me, I can't wrap my head around it. Putting my elbows on the desk, I rest my face in my hands. The luminol isn't going to be enough. I knew that as soon as Cole suggested it. Again, nothing tying the boys to the crime. All I get is a whole bunch of questions I can't answer without getting Cho and Ashleigh involved, not without telling the whole, ugly story. Why should any more lives be ruined in this mess? It doesn't seem fair.

No, at this point, nothing short of a confession will do.

Then it hits me. I shake my head, feeling smart and stupid at the same time. I don't need evidence. I need them to think I have evidence. My mind reels, a plan forming in the back of my thoughts as I shower and change for dinner.

When I head to my room, still wrapped in a green towel, I smell it again, my blood freezing in my veins. I spin, waiting, listening for any sound, for any evidence that it's not all in my head.

There's nothing. Silence and the beating of my own heart. I'm alone and clearly losing my mind. I dress quickly, opting to let my hair air dry into a wavy, brown mess. Opening my bag, I pull out the makeshift camera and put the mini SD card back in the slot, setting it in my window, pointing it out at my room.

"Fool me once," I mutter to myself, adjusting the angle.

I LAUGH HARDER THAN I HAVE IN A LONG TIME AS I watch Derek finish his twentieth hot wing. His black hair hangs long over one eye, the other half of his head shaved short. His black lipstick is smeared across his face, creating an almost Picasso vibe when mixed with the red sauce. Beside him, Kayla readjusts his plastic bib. Her normally wild hair is pulled back into a demure, multi-hued bun. Her face is clean of makeup, making her look fresh-faced and innocent. Derek's eyes water, eyeliner streaking down his cheeks. Reaching across the table, I dab at them with a clean napkin. The last bone bare he tosses on his plate and the waitress, watching in disbelief, hits the bell on the edge of the table.

"Winner!" she shouts, drawing a round of applause from the crowd. Kayla and I whoop loudly. Grabbing for his glass of milk, Derek downs it in one long swallow.

"Dinner is on me," he says, slamming the now-empty glass on the table.

"Way to go, babe," Kayla says, kissing him on the ear.

I look down at my own plate, the last bits of steak piled on the edge, next to the potato remnants. It is the best food I've had in a while, but I'm already bursting at the seams. One more bite might actually kill me.

"Did anyone save room for dessert?" the waitress asks, handing Derek his T-shirt.

We all just look at her and laugh.

"Justin. That figures. It's always the quiet ones," Kayla says when the waitress walks away, stabbing her last bite of grilled salmon. "How are you going to get the police to re-open the case?"

I lean forward, tossing my napkin onto the plate. "I have an idea about that. It's not ideal, but things being what they are, I think it's the only way to prove what happened."

"What can we do?" Derek asks, tearing open a packet of moist wipes.

Sitting back, I shake my head. "Nothing. Not now at any rate. You two are the failsafe. If things go horribly awry, your job is to take everything I have to the cops."

Kayla frowns. "That sounds pretty serious. You're not going to do something stupid, are you?"

Tugging at my ear, I hesitate. "Well, on a scale of one to incredibly stupid, it's a solid seven."

"You're not doing it alone," Derek says. There will be no discussion on that, his tone tells me.

"No, I will need help. I'm going to enlist Cole." They both open their mouths to protest, but I hold up my hands before they can get a word out. "He's both my assistant and my backup, in case I need some muscle. No offence to either of you, but I need someone who can handle themselves in a scuffle, if it comes down to that. I'm really hoping it won't."

Kayla frowns, but nods. "Fine. If there's one thing I *do* trust Cole with, it's keeping you safe."

Derek claps his hands together, "Now that that's settled, who wants to go down to The Circle and ride the Ferris wheel?"

Kayla and I groan in unison.

By the time I get home, it's after ten. The house is dark and I sit in the car for a few minutes, debating whether to go inside. Somehow, going back to Cole's house doesn't seem like a good option. I don't know what his plans are with Courtney, and I don't want to interrupt something.

Moaning, I drop my head, banging it on the steering wheel a few times before getting out of the car and going inside.

The first thing I do is check the SD card. There's no images, which means there was no movement in the house while I was gone. I put the card back in and set it aside. Maybe I really am just losing it. Maybe the stress of staying alone is really too much. I'd spent Dad's last deployment at Kayla's house. But three months as a houseguest gets old fast, and this was just supposed to be a short stint, a month, six weeks at the most. Even so.

Slipping into my soft cotton pajama pants and purple tank top, I shuffle out to the living room, flipping on the stereo and settling into the sofa with my well-loved copy of *Hitchhikers Guide to the Galaxy*. The sound of my front door jiggling makes me jump. I'd remembered to lock it, thank goodness. My chest constricts, and I hold my breath. Finally, there's a gentle tap. Setting the book down, I move to the door and see Cole's face through the peephole.

Opening the door quickly, I pull him inside. His lip is split and swollen, the side of his face red, a welt forming.

"What happened?" I demand, immediately

looking him over for more damage.

He shakes his head. "I'm fine."

I cock my head to the side and point to the sofa. "Sit down; I'll get the first aid kit."

He obeys, his shoulders slumped, but as he sits, he hollers. "I'm okay, really."

But I've already retrieved the tackle-box sized first aid kit from the kitchen, and I take a seat across from him on the coffee table. Pulling out a long Q-tip with Betadine on the end, I move to clean the cut first. My hands hover for a moment. "This may sting," I say, and before he can protest, I gently swab the cut. He hisses and I lean forward, blowing on it gently, the way my mom used to when cleaning my skinned knees.

His face falls slack and I lean back, cleaning up the wound with a dry gauze pad. Tipping his chin to the side, I reach up, touching his temple softly. It's not bad, but there's going to be one hell of a lump in the morning.

"That feels good," he murmurs. "Your hands are cold."

"Want an ice pack?" I ask.

"No." he exhales deeply. Reaching up, he takes my hand in his, pressing it to the lump. "This is fine. This is good."

I sigh. "What happened?" I wait, expecting a heroic tale of Cole taking on a purse snatcher or fighting off a drunken biker.

"I broke up with Courtney," he answers.

I frown, not understanding.

He continues. "She punched me in the face."

To my credit, I manage not to laugh. It's hard and I have to focus on holding my face neutral. It's not funny really. Or so I keep telling myself. "That explains the lip, but what about this?" I ask, gently rubbing his temple.

"Um, as I was leaving, she threw a shoe at me."

"A shoe?"

"Yeah, one of those tall, thick ones."

"A wedge?" The first of the giggles begin to bubble inside me.

"Yeah," he says, watching my face closely.

Pressing my lips together, I fight not to laugh. It physically hurts.

Dropping my hand, he rolls his eyes. "Its fine, you can laugh if you want to."

I press my fingers to my mouth and shake my head. "No, I'm sorry. It's not funny. I'm sorry you broke up." Quickly packing the kit back up, I stand, taking it to the bookshelf.

"It was bound to happen. You were right, what you said at the beach," he says softly.

My eyes fall on a picture in a silver frame. It's my mom on her wedding day, smiling so widely that she radiates joy. "No, I wasn't. You have enough hard stuff in your life. Who can blame you for wanting one thing to be simple?"

"It just," he hesitates, "it wasn't fair. Not to either of us. She deserves to be with someone who is crazy about her. I'm just crazy."

Still staring at the picture, I feel something wash over me. Courage, maybe. Stupidity, definitely.

"You know, my mom told me something once. She said that life is too short for cheap chocolate, ugly shoes, and for loving people halfway." I bite my lip until my eyes begin to water. "Thing is, she was right." I have to force the next words from my throat. Squeezing my eyes closed, I take a deep breath. "Thing is, I'm in love with you. And I know it's messy and complicated and let's face it, my timing is awful, but there it is. I didn't tell you before because the idea of losing you, of losing what we have now, scares the shit out of me. But not telling you, not saying the words out loud, it hurts. Keeping it in hurts." I open my eyes and he's frozen, unmoving. I sit back down across from him.

"If you don't feel the same way, I get it. But I had to say it out loud, at least once." He says nothing, his expression surprised. *It's now or never*, I hear a voice in the back of my mind whisper. Slowly, waiting for him to stop me at any moment, I lean forward, slip my hands around his neck, and kiss him.

He kisses me back, or at least I think he does. When I pull away, his expression is serene. He's looking at me like I'm his favorite thing in the world. Mustering my courage, I lean forward again, but this time, I step forward, straddling him, sitting on his lap and pressing him back against the couch. His arms snake around my waist, tightening as I lower my lips to his again. Trying to be careful of the cut, I move gently, taking his top lip between mine. He moans once, and I'm sure I've hurt him. Pulling away, I cup his face in my hands.

His hands grasp my sides, and he shakes his head. "Wait. I just need to breathe for a minute." I rock back just a bit, but he doesn't release me. "What are you doing here?" he asks, his voice hoarse.

"Something I've wanted to do for a really long time," I answer. "I'm sorry. Should I not have?"

He doesn't answer, and I try to scramble off his lap. It's too soon. I've mistaken his friendship for something else. I've ruined everything.

He holds me tight. "No. I mean yes." He sighs. "You shouldn't have. I should have. I've wanted to do that from the moment I laid eyes on you."

I don't ask what stopped him. I know, because it's the same thing that stopped me. Fear. Circumstances. *Life.* "Then why aren't you kissing me right now?" I ask, leaning forward again.

Releasing my waist, he takes my face in his hands. "Everything in my head is tangled up in knots. I can't tell if you're unraveling me or just pulling my strings," he says, licking his bottom lip.

"Not to freak you out, but I'm pretty sure that's what love is," I answer, holding his gaze.

This time, he pulls me close, kissing me roughly. His hands are on my neck, in my hair, running down my back. I can't breathe, can't think. A heartbeat hammers in my ears, and I don't know if it's mine or his. Standing, he lifts me into the air. I wrap my legs around his waist. He carries me to my room, then sits on my bed, me still sitting on his lap. I feel him stiffen and I pull back, my breath ragged.

"I'm way out of your league," I say, smiling.

He grins, tracing my jaw with his fingertips. "That's true."

"And I'm way too smart to date a guy like you."

"That's also true."

I press our foreheads together. "It's going to be hard and it's going to be messy and it's going to be complicated. Can you handle that?"

"As long as I get to be with you, I can handle that."

"Good." I smirk. "Because it's also going to be totally worth it."

Leaning back, I strip off my tank top, my hands shaking and uncertain, then I grab the hem of his shirt and lift it over his head, tossing it carelessly to the floor. I've seen him shirtless a dozen times before, but this feels different. I run a hand down his chest, reveling at the texture of his skin beneath my fingers. I'm quaking like a fault line, every fiber of me tingling with fear, with anticipation.

I hope he doesn't notice.

He kisses me again, rolling me onto my back,

and the uncertainty is driven away in a rush of heat. This isn't some daydream. This is real. This is happening. The weight of him on top of me is exquisite, goose bumps blossoming across my bare skin while sensations, foreign and indefinable, rage inside me. He kisses his way between my breasts and down my stomach. Each time his warm lips touch my skin, something inside me winds, tighter and tighter, aching for release. I'm a bomb, just waiting to go off. Then, grabbing the waistband of my pants, he tugs them off. When he looks down at me, I have to fight the urge to cover myself. I'm exposed—raw and aching. He swears under his breath.

"My God, you are so beautiful," he says, fumbling with the fly of his jeans. "Are you sure about this?"

In response, I arch beneath him. I don't want to speak; I don't trust my voice anymore. Despite the sheer, unadulterated terror, I've never been so sure of anything in my life. I want him on me, inside me, consuming me before I burst into flames. I didn't know it would be like this, *could* be like this. When he returns to my arms, only the flimsy fabric of our underwear separates us. The realization makes me shudder, and he holds me tighter. I should probably tell him it's my first time. Will he know? Will he be able to tell? The coiling inside me worsens, driving away the thoughts. My mouth is swollen and tender from his kisses. I want more; I want to lose myself in him and never stop to find myself. It's only when

I feel him, hard and ready against my thigh, that a sliver of the real world sneaks in.

"Do you have a condom?" I whisper in his ear as he kisses my neck.

When he sighs, I have my answer. "No. I don't suppose you do?"

It's so funny that it's sad. I snap my fingers. "Fresh out."

Just like that, reality crashes back in and we are both laughing at the sheer absurdity of it all.

"I could go to the store?" he offers.

Winding my fingers into his hair, I shake my head. "I don't think I could handle you leaving me like this."

"So... we just wait then. We've waited this long," he says, kissing my neck again. "Another day or two won't kill me. I think. I hope."

"Yeah," I say. "But you'll still stay, right?"

Rolling off me, he props himself up on one elbow. "It would take a nuclear blast to get me out of this bed."

He traces the length of me with his fingertips, making me flush over and over. I do the same, exploring him, memorizing every rise and fall, every curve of his body as he growls in frustration. Practically leaping from the bed, he rakes his hand through his hair.

"What are you doing?" I ask, suddenly afraid I've done something wrong.

"I'm going to go take a cold shower. You," he points at me, "you should put some clothes on before I get back."

Muttering something under his breath, he stalks out of the room, leaving me to fight back the heat boiling inside me. By the time he finishes, I'm back in my pajamas, lying across my bed. He's in his borrowed sweatpants, bare-chested and glistening as he rubs the towel across his head, drying his hair.

"Well, that's not fair," I tease, staring at him from my pillow.

Tossing the towel aside and flicking my light off, he crawls in bed. "Shut up and go to sleep, Farris."

I nestle into him, curling up against his chest as he puts his arms around me. I want to make a smart-ass remark, but I'm suddenly bone tired, warm, and content. Before I realize it, I'm drifting off, the sound of his breathing lulling me to sleep.

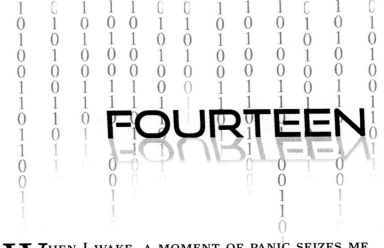

FOURTEEN

WHEN I WAKE, A MOMENT OF PANIC SEIZES ME. Blinking, I look up into Cole's still-sleeping face. Will he regret last night? Did we make a terrible mistake?

"You shouldn't think so hard this early in the morning," he mumbles, cradling me against him.

I grin. Then I bolt upright. "What time is it?"

He rolls onto his back languidly. "Calm down, it's only after six."

I rake a hand through my hair. "Mondays are of the devil."

Sitting up behind me, Cole kisses my shoulder. "We could ditch out, stay here. Do... whatever."

Craning my neck, I kiss him, slowly, deeply, with a promise of things yet to come. "Tempting as that is," I say, pulling back, "I have a test today."

He whines. "Make it up tomorrow."

It's a tempting offer. Hell, it's beyond tempting. But some stupid, nagging voice in my head tells me to be responsible. I hate that voice. "What's your work schedule like this week?" I ask, crawling over him and out of bed.

"I close tonight, off tomorrow and Wednesday, then I work till nine Thursday and Friday. Why?"

Walking over to my closet, I stand on one foot. "Because I have an idea for getting Justin to confess. But I'm gonna need you there."

I don't hear him get out of bed, but suddenly, his arms are around me and he's rocking me gently from behind. "Good. I was afraid I'd have to fight to get you to take me with you." He spins me around in his arms, tipping my chin up with his finger. "Because I don't want you anywhere near Justin or Cody without me. Okay? I'm serious."

Stretching up on my tiptoes, I give him a quick kiss. "I promise. Now get out, I gotta get dressed."

Releasing me, he balks. "For real? I just saw you naked not seven hours ago."

I blush. "Not naked. Not totally. And it doesn't matter because I want to get dressed in private. So scram. Go make yourself useful and make coffee or something."

With a grumble, he turns and stalks out of my room, closing the door behind him. For some stupid reason, I can't decide what to wear. I stare into the closet like it's the portal to freaking Narnia and hope a satyr pops out with the perfect blouse. Once the smell of freshly brewing coffee wafts in, all bets are off. I grab a pair of jeans and a jade-green tank top with lace at the bottom, pull a threadbare vintage Superman T-shirt on over it, and head for the kitchen, stopping to stuff my bare feet into a pair of white low-top Chucks. Cole is standing in the kitchen, dressed in yesterday's jeans and T-shirt.

"We should probably run by your house and grab you some clean clothes," I offer, getting two mugs down.

Moving so fast I never see it coming, Cole grabs me by the waist, driving me against the wall and kissing me like he wants to swallow me whole. When he finally stops, I'm gasping for breath. His forehead is pressed against mine, his eyes closed.

"How am I supposed to focus on anything now?" His hands knead the flesh of my sides gently, his fingers slipping under my shirt. "All I can think about is kissing you."

His voice is ragged, strained. Reaching up, I touch his lip, the tiny cut Courtney left there. "I don't know, think of baseball? Dead kittens? What hot dogs are made of?"

He chuckles, opening his eyes. "I love you." As soon as the words escape his mouth, he freezes, as if shocked by his own admission.

"I love you too," I say. "But you already knew that."

He visibly relaxes, the smile on his face softening. "I think I did, actually."

COLE'S MOM IS, THANKFULLY, AT WORK WHEN I DROP him off to get some clean clothes. He's stayed over a dozen times before, but the idea of facing his mom after last night makes me queasy. It will be written all over my face, and she will hate me forever, I just know it. With a long kiss goodbye, I leave him, knowing he needs to take his own car to school since he has to go straight to work after eighth period.

As soon as I show up, Kayla rushes over. I brace myself, knowing I can't hide anything from her. Sure enough, she stops dead in her tracks, in the middle of the parking lot.

"Oh my God, you did it." Her eyes narrow. "You let Cole finger-bang you, didn't you?"

Closing the distance in three long strides, I grab her by the arm. "We did not do it, and you can't say finger-bang. We're in a YA novel for shit's sake."

She jerks her arm free, lowering her voice. "I want details, and I want them now."

Behind her, Derek makes a face.

"Ok, first off, no. No details. But, I will say that Cole and Courtney broke up. He came over afterward and... we... um..."

She makes a face.

"No," I say again. "But we are, I mean, I think, we are *together* now. Like, a couple."

"Say the word. I want to hear you say it," she demands, her pigtails flying as she shakes her head.

"Boyfriend," I say finally. "He's my boyfriend."

Derek drapes an arm across my shoulder. "Now was that so hard?"

Kayla nudges him. "Hey, she said no details. Have some friggin' respect."

I burst out laughing, Derek just looks uncomfortable, and Kayla smirks. Walking together to my locker, we pass Courtney. She doesn't look at me, but I can feel hate radiating off her like heat waves off a summer sidewalk.

Cole is already waiting for me there. I'm about to tell him to play it cool, the last thing I want is to rub our new relationship in Courtney's face, but it's too late. Taking my hand, he pulls me into his chest and kisses the top of my head.

"Dude, what happened to your face?" Kayla blurts out.

As expected, the lump on Cole's temple has turned a vivid shade of black-purple and the cut on his lip is an angry red. He leans over to me. "On a scale of one to ten, how much do I have to tell them?"

"Courtney threw a shoe at him when he broke up with her," I answer for him.

"Youch," Derek says, then, glancing across the hall at the redhead, he shrugs. "All things considered, you probably got off easy."

"Yep, because that's nothing compared to what I'll do to your face if you hurt my girl, savvy?" Kayla says, pointing her finger at Cole.

He raises both hands. "Got it."

Derek adds, "Yeah, because there would be a line, and I would be in it."

"You two probably aren't the only ones," Cole says, half grinning and nudging me. "Not that there would be much left of me when she was done."

Bringing my shoulder to my chin, I bat my eyelashes innocently. Wrapping his arms around me, he pulls me in for a kiss on the tip of my nose. "Good luck on your test today. Which you didn't study for, slacker."

"I've been a little busy, what with all the murder solving, breaking and entering—"

Kayla cuts me off. "Boyfriend stealing."

"Hey," I snap.

But Cole takes the snark in stride. "You can't steal what was always yours," he says flatly. "See you at lunch."

Releasing me, he heads down the hall. I watch him walk away, realizing for the first time that he's mine. Really truly. That gorgeous chunk of man-meat belongs to me. Tucking a strand of hair behind my ear and giving myself a gentle shake, I head for class.

As it turns out, the test is postponed anyway. Our teacher is out with the flu and our sub, an insanely good-looking guy with wavy, brown hair and broad shoulders, has us work on a project instead. It's supposed to be a goof assignment, plan the perfect bank robbery with a local credit union as the target. Unfortunately for him, he okays the use of electronics. After a speedy hack of the county records office, I have the assignment done. I hand it in without saying a word and he glances over the paper, then back up at me.

"What's this?"

"The perfect robbery," I say categorically.

"This isn't a bank robbery. This is a private residence."

"It's the bank manager's house, actually. You break in, load some malware to his phone that records and filters the information from the accelerometer through a database and sends the information back to you. He takes the phone to work, sets it on his desk, and enters his log-in information. Boom. You have access to the entire mainframe." I frown. "Welcome to the digital world."

"This would actually work," he says, staring at me. His expression isn't surprised as much as impressed.

I nod, looking down at the desk. He's leaning on it, his fists supporting him as he reads over the paper again. His blue button-down shirt is rolled up at the sleeves, displaying a rather impressive forearm tattoo for a teacher. That's when the smell hits me.

Every muscle in my body goes rigid, my mind reeling. *It has to be a coincidence*, I tell myself. Maybe I'm even imagining it. I inhale deeply.

No, it's the same, the same smell from my room. My eyes flick up to his face. He's young, mid-twenties maybe, with a square face and thick neck. From the single undone button in his shirt, I see the beginning of what I'm sure is an impressive set of chest muscles.

He's either the buffest teacher in history, or he's some flavor of military. I take an involuntary step back. "Can I go to the nurse?" I ask. "I'm not feeling great."

He nods once, handing the paper back to me.

I practically run from the room into the hall. I swear its thirty degrees cooler out there. Slinging my backpack over my shoulder, I head for the health office.

While I'm sitting in the tiny, white closet of a room, waiting for the nurse to arrive, I spy a bowl of brightly colored foil-wrapped condoms on her desk. Looking around, making sure no one else is looking, I grab a handful and stuff them in my bag, feeling like a cross between a thief and a moron. Why does being safe have to feel so damn awkward?

Just as I zip up my bag, Mr. Keiser, the PE teacher, walks in. "Mrs. Johnson is over at the middle school today doing sex ed. Is there something I can help you with?"

There's only one fast, efficient way to get out of here. "It's the cramps," I whine, holding my torso. "It's like I'm being stabbed in the ovaries."

He falters. "Do you just need to go home and rest?"

I nod, looking as pathetic as possible. He scribbles me a check-out pass and I head for my car, texting Cole as I go. *Test was a bust. Had a sub. I'm going home, not feeling great.*

I knew we should have ditched. You okay?

I'll live. Bring me lunch?

Sure thing.

I shoot a similar text off to Kayla and hop in my car, allowing myself a moment to bask in the warmth of the sun streaming onto my dashboard before driving home.

FIFTEEN

I'M ELBOW DEEP IN SOCIAL MEDIA PAGES WHEN COLE finally arrives, sack of burgers in hand.

"You realize that the point of leaving school is to quit doing work, right?"

Standing, I greet him with a kiss, distracting him while I grab the food and then ducking under his arm and heading for the kitchen table. "Side project. You know me. I can't sit still for too long."

"Which reminds me." He holds up a finger, going back to the front door and returning with a package. "This was on your porch."

I glance at the sticker while I plate up two burgers. "It's the luminol. I had it overnight shipped."

"Efficient."

"Just ready for all this to be over," I say, sliding his plate to him. He dumps a container of fries on both plates, and we dig in.

"Speaking of, do you have SAT prep this week?" I ask, taking a huge bite, a dribble of ketchup sliding down my chin.

"Nope. I did mine over the summer. Why?"

I wipe my face. "Well, I think my dad might be getting back early. I was thinking of meeting him at the airfield, surprising him. And I was wondering if you'd come with me."

His eyes narrow. "This feels like a trap."

I grin, holding up my hands. "No traps. I just thought, he'd be so happy to be home..."

"That he wouldn't be quite so pissed that his little girl is dating, well, me."

"Not quite what I meant, but basically."

He stuffs a fry in his mouth. "If you want me there, I'm there. As long as I don't have to work."

"See, first day on the job and you're nailing this boyfriend thing."

He chuckles. "I feel like we should have a sign, like they have in factories. It's been blank days since Cole's last screw-up."

"Signage approved. Let's talk bonuses," I say, wagging my eyebrows.

"If I didn't have to go back to class, I'd be all over that offer." His grin widens. "Raincheck? Tomorrow night maybe?"

Frowning, I look down at my plate. "Actually, we're going to be a little tied up tomorrow night."

"I can't decide if I hope you're being literal or not," he says, wiping his hands on his jeans.

Pushing the plate aside, I break down my plan. To his credit, he lets me finish before folding his arms across his chest.

"That's a terrible plan."

"It's a good plan, and you know it."

"Using yourself as bait is never a good plan," he adds, shaking his head.

"You'll be right there the whole time. If you have a better idea, I'm all ears."

He puckers his lips, sitting back and stretching out his legs. Finally, he sighs. "Fine. We do it your way. But you need to be careful. Promise me. I'll be nearby, but if he hurts you, I'll be the one going to jail for murder. Because I'll kill him."

"You're cute when you're worried," I say, leaning over and putting a hand on his knee.

"Then something tells me I'll be *cute* a lot with you around."

Then, in a move I never see coming, he grabs me, lifting me to my feet and carrying me to the couch in the living room, where he proceeds to kiss me until I've completely forgotten everything else. I barely have the strength to kick him out in time to get him back to work. Once he's gone, the sensation of his hands on my skin is haunting, the warmth fading slowly from my body.

Kayla shows up a little after five with a bleach kit and some color dye. I let her bleach streaks in my hair, adding more strands of vibrant blue into my chestnut locks while we watch the latest episode of *Scream* on TV.

"Come on, how did no one see that coming?" I complain, my head foiled like a baked potato. "I knew who the killer was weeks ago."

Beside me, Kayla rolls her eyes. "Yes, Sherlock. Your keen deductive skills are unmatched." She pauses. "Wait, if you're Sherlock, does that make me Watson?"

"Depends, can I be the hot British Sherlock, and you still be cool Lucy Lu Watson?"

"Of course."

"Then yes. You're for sure my Watson. Now make yourself useful and go make some popcorn while I go rinse out my head," I say, pulling myself off the floor with the arm of the sofa.

"Butter Blast or Cheesey?" she calls down the hall.

"Surprise me," I answer, turning on the water and climbing into the shower.

A few minutes later, mid-lather, I hear the bathroom door open. Peeking out the curtain, I see Kayla slide up onto the vanity. "Ok, for real though. I want to hear about you and Cole," she says, flipping nonchalantly through her phone.

I go back to washing and rinsing. "I told you I was into him."

"I know. And that I get, I really do. He's got that whole bad-boy James Dean vibe going for him." She hesitates. "What I don't understand is how you can trust him not to treat you like he has his other girls.

You said it yourself, he's a loyal friend, but he's a terrible boyfriend."

"Can we talk about this when I'm out of the shower?"

"No, this is better. People tend to be more honest when they're naked," she says decidedly.

"I guess, I don't. I mean, I know he has a pattern with girls. But I also think, I think that you teach people how to treat you. If you accept shit, people give you shit. If you demand better, then they either give you better or they get lost."

She sighs. "I just don't want you going into this thinking that you can change him. In my experience, people don't really change."

"I don't want him to change. I fell for him knowing his flaws perfectly well. And he knows mine."

"And you aren't afraid he's going to hurt you, in the end?"

That makes me pause, mostly because I hadn't given that too much thought. But if you begin something being afraid of the end, how can you enjoy the middle?

"I guess I can't really think about that. All I can do is make sure that every minute is worth it, whatever happens."

"He's a senior. In two months, he'll be graduating. Going off to whatever..."

I don't answer. What can I say? I have enough credits to graduate early, but it will still be next spring. Is he planning to go off to college? Stay here and work at the pizza factory forever? I never asked, because it never really made a difference before. But now...

When I don't say anything, she continues. "I'm not saying I think you should break it off. Just...just be careful. I worry about you."

I rinse the last of the conditioner from my hair. "Why is everyone always so worried about me?" I ask. "I'm not a moron, nor am I incapable of taking care of myself."

"You're smart, probably the smartest person I've ever known," she says. "But sometimes, you have a hard time seeing the things closest to you. You're an all-or-nothing, leap-before-you-look kind of person. And on top of that, you're a fixer. You carry the weight of the world on your shoulders and you're still the first one through the door to save someone. I just want you to know that sometimes, it's okay if you can't fix everything. It's okay if you can only save one person. And it's okay if that person is you."

Kayla is long gone before Cole returns. I'm already in bed, lying on top of the covers, window wide open, with a gentle breeze ticking my skin. When I hear him come in and close the door behind him, I sit up on my elbow. He peeks in my bedroom door.

"I half expected you to be face deep in keyboard,"

he says.

I hold out my hand to him. "Are you staying over?"

"If you want me to."

"I do," I admit.

He enters the room, taking my hand. I pull him onto the bed beside me. He kisses me gently, his fingers weaving through my hair. "This is fun," he says, plucking out a strand of blue.

"Kayla."

"I figured. Hey, are you alright? You seem a little... off."

I chew my lip. I don't want to talk about the future. I don't want to dwell on the maybe tomorrows. I don't want to lose this moment. Tracing his face with my fingertips, I answer, "Have you ever wanted to hold onto a moment so badly you tried to memorize it in perfect detail, so you knew you would have it forever?"

His expression is soft, genuine. I love seeing this look on his face. I'm pretty sure it's something he keeps just for me, this raw vulnerability, the honest core of him.

"The first time I stayed over, we were watching that movie and you fell asleep on my shoulder. I carried you to bed. There was this strand of hair that fell in your face." He smiles, "You looked so peaceful, so content. I don't think I've ever seen something so beautiful. I just sat here and stared at you for the longest time. I wanted to take it in, to capture it. Because I knew that it wouldn't last. I knew that I'd always be yours and you'd never be mine."

His words are so tender that they make my heart ache. There are a million things I want to say, but something holds me back. Instead, I touch the side of his face. "My God, do you ever get tired of being so wrong all the time?" I laugh.

"I've never been so glad to be wrong." He kisses me again. "I'm going to go get cleaned up."

"I'll be here."

By the time he showers and returns in a fresh pair of shorts, I'm drifting off. He curls up next to me, draping an arm across my waist. I nuzzle him, and he kisses the top of my head. "Get some rest. Tomorrow's going to be one helluva day," he whispers.

I WAKE TO THE HISS OF BACON FRYING AND REACH out, pulling the empty pillow close, inhaling the unmistakable scent of Cole. Dressing quickly, I head for the kitchen. Cole is just plating up the food, scrambled eggs, toast, and turkey bacon.

"What's all this?" I ask, taking a seat and admiring the spread. He sets a mug of coffee in front of me and I snatch it up, blowing across the top.

"What kind of boyfriend would I be if I let my girlfriend go catch a killer on an empty stomach?"

he asks, his tone light. "But really, I just realized this morning that your dad's going to be back in a few days. I don't think he's going to let these little sleepovers continue, especially now."

I tap the side of the mug with my fingernail. He has a point. I feel myself frown. I'm going to miss having him around, miss having coffee with him in the morning, and miss falling asleep with him at night.

"It's going to be okay," he says, stroking my cheek with one finger. "Just different. We don't have much of this left, so I figured we should enjoy it while we can."

Setting the cup down, I pick up my fork. "About that. What are your post-graduation plans?" I try to sound calm, not at all freaked out about the prospect of him leaving.

"College, for sure. I got accepted to a few good schools and Mom would kill me if I didn't at least try. What about you? Big plans for post-grad life?"

I stab a forkful of eggs, moving it around my plate but not eating. My stomach is tumbling like a dryer and the thought of putting food in it suddenly makes me queasy.

"I can't graduate until spring," I say. "But I'm sure I'll end up a computer science major somewhere. Nothing definite yet."

Reaching over, he grabs the legs of my chair and spins it so I'm looking at him. "Hey, if you're worried about me leaving, don't be. I'm not going anywhere without you. The great thing about not having a major decided is that I can do general ed classes pretty much anywhere. So, as long as you don't mind me following you around for a while longer..."

He doesn't finish the thought because I'm already in his lap, my arms draped over his shoulders as I kiss him. When he finally pulls me back, we're both breathless.

"Ok, if we keep doing this, we're not going to make it to school at all."

Knowing he's right, I climb off him and back into my chair, forcing down a few bites of breakfast and draining the coffee.

He drives us to school and kisses me goodbye at my locker before first period. Kayla watches us warily. As soon as he's gone, we head to first period.

"I'll say this for the boy, I haven't seen you look this happy in a long time," she says, turning into her class.

I smirk at her comment. I haven't felt this good in a while, so it's no surprise that it shows. As soon as I turn the corner into my own classroom, I come face to face with Courtney, her red hair carefully French braided down one side of her head, the other side left loose in a mess of strawberry waves. I fully expect her to lose it, to yell and make a scene, but she doesn't. She just glares daggers at me as I slide past, taking my seat.

During class, my eyes keep sliding over to her, but she doesn't acknowledge me. When class ends, I stand, pretty sure I've escaped her wrath.

"I need to say something to you." Courtney's voice catches me off-guard.

SIXTEEN

"**O**K," I SAY HESITANTLY, SCOOPING UP MY BAG. "I just want you to know that I wanted to be your friend. Not because of Cole, but because... I could see how you were with them. The way you defended them and stood by them. I'm pretty sure any one of my friends would stab me in the back for a Klondike Bar." She hesitates, shifting her weight. "I guess I was jealous of that as much as anything."

"So, you don't want to stab my eyes out with an ice pick?"

She shrugs. "Well, yeah, I kinda do. But I realized that I'm not nearly as upset about losing Cole as I am about losing the chance to be your friend. So, I guess what I'm saying is, if it's not too weird, do you want to hang out sometime? Go shopping or catch a movie or something?"

I almost drop my bag. "Yeah. Sure. I'd like that," I fumble.

"Cool," she says, flipping her hair over her shoulder and stalking out into the hall.

Derek slides into the room behind her. "What was that?" he asks, his hands stuffed in the pockets of his baggy, black pants.

I run my tongue across my teeth the way you do when you've just taken a bite of something way too sweet. "I think my boyfriend's ex-girlfriend just asked me on a date."

"That is so your life," he says, pulling out a slip of paper. "Here, Justin's cell number. Compliments of Ashleigh. She did ask why you needed it, but I feigned ignorance."

"Probably best. She's going to be pretty pissed when the truth comes out. I still don't get it though," I say, taking the number and plugging it into my phone.

"What's that?"

I jerk my head, and we walk out into the hallway together. "Either Justin wanted Ashleigh enough to kill Mac, in which case, why stop there? Why not kill Cody too? Or pin the murder on him? Or, Cody killed Mac, in which case, why wouldn't Justin go to the cops? Then he's free to be with Ashleigh. It's just not adding up."

"It's love, Farris, not math. It doesn't have to add up. Emotions are volatile and unpredictable, not chemical reactions with reliable outcomes. That's why they are called *crimes of passion* and not *crimes of perfect reason*."

I shake my head. "Fair enough."

I spend most of lunch hold up in the chemistry lab, preparing a solution for the powdered luminol. Cole guards the door behind me as I pour the contents of the solution into the spray bottle. "I'll have to add the powder last, it's only good for four hours after I mix it into the solution," I say, rummaging through the teacher's desk for the UV blacklight flashlight I remember him keeping in there. "Score."

I hold it up victoriously.

"You sure this will work?" he asks.

"I sure as hell hope so, it's our only shot," I say as we sneak back down to my locker and put the spray bottle inside. Pulling out my phone, I send the text to Justin, masking my own number.

I know what you did. Meet me at the pool at 6 tonight and it can all go away.

"You sure he'll take the bait?" Cole asks, wrapping his arms around me.

"He was willing to cover up the crime, if not commit it outright. He'll do whatever it takes to keep it under wraps," I say, hoping I sound more confident than I feel.

SEVENTEEN

AFTER SCHOOL, COLE AND I HIDE OUT IN THE SMALL stage prop house in the auditorium until all the students and janitors have cleared out for the day. It'll be easier than trying to break in again, and it gives us time to go over the plan again. Carefully mixing the luminol, I shine the UV light on the bottle and it glows bright yellow-green.

At about quarter till six, he heads to the gym, propping open the back doors with a chunk of wood. With a quick, urgent kiss, I release him to go do his part and I head back to my locker to grab my tablet.

When I slam it shut, Justin is already there, leaning against it. "Shit," I say. "What are you, half ninja?"

He smirks. "Something like that. What are you doing here?"

I cradle my tablet to my chest, trying not to let my panic show. "Same thing as you, I'd imagine."

He sighs, shaking his head. "You know, I really hoped it wasn't you."

"Yeah, the feeling is mutual."

He rubs his face in one hand, and then pushes off the locker. "So, you wanna tell me what all this is about?"

"I have a problem, and you seem like the problem-solving sort," I say, trying to hold my chin up high.

He laughs dryly. "Whatever, I'm out of here."

"I know what you did, and I have proof. You walk away now, and I go straight to the cops," I say, not having to feign desperation.

Turning back to me, his eyes narrow. "What proof?"

I frown and jerk my head. He follows me to the pool. "I have to admit, I don't quite get it," I admit. "I mean, I don't get why you did it."

Taking the luminol from my bag and setting the tablet on top, I begin walking around the pool, squirting the liquid with one hand and shining the light with the other. "There are three things you forgot," I say, trying to get him talking.

"Please, enlighten me," he says, folding his arms across his chest.

"Well, first off, it's just, head wounds, man, they bleed and bleed. Even the minor ones." As soon as the words are out, I hit the edge of the blood trace and the ground lights up like a rave. I keep spraying, outlining the entire blood pool for him to see. "And second, this is a salt water pool, not chlorine. It doesn't clean up blood the way chlorine would. I bet there's enough trace in this concrete to get DNA."

The doors to the pool fly open and Cody strides in, still in his ROTC uniform. I freeze. His arrival throws a kink in things, big time. I chew on my lip, praying Cole is close, that he made it to his position in time. Cody walks up beside Justin, who is barely ten feet from me, and puts a hand on his shoulder. The look they exchange is familiar, *intimate*, and reality crashes in on me.

"Okay, that makes more sense," I say, turning my back on them and shaking my head. "I couldn't figure out why you guys would kill Mac. I thought it was because you found out she'd been screwing around with him, and it was just a rage thing. I mean, I saw the videos and wow. Just wow. I didn't even like the girl, and I was kinda pissed." I glance over my shoulder, and they are both staring at me blankly. My pulse picks up, my mouth going dry. I lick my lips. "Sorry, boyfriends are always the last to know, I guess. Though, on the scale of shitty secrets to keep from someone, I think you two totally take the cake on that. So what, did you two sneak away from the dance for a private make-out session at the pool? Mac walked in and..." The pieces fall into place in my head like tumblers in a lock. I walk over to the wall and start spraying the rescue hook, hoping they don't notice how my hand shakes as I do.

"And you just couldn't bear for your little secret to get out, right? What would your parents say?

What would your friends say? Wait, don't answer any of that. I don't care. I do wonder what the plan was though. Get your wings, have a successful career for a while, marry the poster princess for conservative rights, then go into politics? All while having a secret affair with your childhood friend." I wave my hand. "I feel like it's been done. I mean, it's kind of so cliché that it borders on comical. But Mac didn't see it that way, did he? Maybe he threatened you or tried to blackmail you. He was going to tell Ashleigh at a minimum. You fought. He hit his head. Which of you tossed him into the pool?"

Cody steps forward. "We don't know what you're talking about."

I make an as-if face and shine the light on the wall. "Sure you do. See, blood isn't the only thing salt water won't wash away. Fingerprints are also pesky to clean up. And I'm guessing yours are all over this." That's not strictly true, but I'm hoping they don't know that. The tip of the hook lights up with blood residue. "And, of course, there's the evidence I'm sure you still have in your trunk, unless you bleached that out? Or did you toss him in Justin's truck bed? Funny thing about that... there are all kinds of crevices for evidence to hide in a truck bed, even if you hose it out." Again, I'm probably giving the police forensics' team way too much credit, but I'm hoping they've seen enough TV shows to be afraid I'm telling the truth.

Justin grabs Cody's arm, and Cody shrugs it off.

Breathing out slowly, I force myself to keep calm, to keep going. I'm not there yet, but I almost have them. I can feel it. The first cracks are forming. "That's the problem, though. You thought you got away with it, so you just quit covering your tracks. I bet you didn't even wipe the location-tracking data off your phone." Justin pales, a look of absolute panic washing across his face. I keep pressing. "You know—that little hidden feature that sends you push notifications and helps you find theaters or restaurants close by? It also provides a map of where you went and when you went there. Time-stamped GPS."

I take a small bow. "See, technology, it's kind of my thing. So when Justin opened my *I know what you did last summer* text, I infected his phone with malware. Now all that pesky map data is copied and on my tablet. All I have to do is hand it over."

Cody lowers his head, slowly closing the gap between us. "Then do it," he challenges.

My heart races. I glance back at Justin, who looks like he's about to lose his lunch. He's the weak link, and I have to press it now or I'm going to get nothing.

"What do you think, Justin? Do you think Cody will stick up for you? Will he have your back? Or do you think he'll let you take the fall alone? I mean, this life, this easy, fake life he wants, the one he's willing to kill for, do you think it means more to him than you do?" I turn my gaze back to Cody. "Afraid they won't welcome an openly gay cadet at the Academy? I hear they have a policy about that now."

Justin shakes his head. "Ashleigh's Dad is alumni. It's his recommendation that's getting him in."

I hold up one hand, pointing the spray bottle at Cody for emphasis. "Well, you said it yourself, Justin. Some people can't handle complication. I'm betting Cody's willing to leave you twisting in the wind. Hell, he might throw you under the bus himself. It's a good story, obsessed friend kills romantic rival. I bet the police are dumb enough to buy that. Or maybe it *was* you. Maybe you saw that Mac was unconscious after the fight, so you rolled him into the pool. Did you hope he was already dead? Did you watch him drown?"

He cracks, exploding in sheer terror. "No, I didn't. Cody was the one. He did it. It was his idea to dump the body. He said if anyone knew, if anyone found out—"

Cody silences him, but it's too late. "Shut the fuck up, man. I'm serious."

I sag in relief. Bending over, Cody picks up my tablet from my bag. "That tracking info, it's all on this?" With a flick, he tosses it into the pool. Then he takes a step forward, gesturing to the blood. "And as far as all this, thanks for the cleaning tips. We'll do a better job this time."

This is it. The moment he decides that his secret is worth more than my life. I see it in his eyes, a flicker of resignation. He's already killed one person and gotten away with it—what's one more? He's probably already planning my story. Accident? A slip and fall into the pool maybe. He takes one more step, and the luminol and the flashlight fall from my hand. Every muscle in my body tenses. I've only taken a handful of self-defense classes, and I know there's no way I'm any match for Cody, much less the two of them. But there's also no way in hell I'm going down without a fight.

"You forgot about the third thing," I say, my voice almost a growl.

He steps forward again, unimpressed with my threat. "And what is that?"

I point at the ceiling. "You forgot about the cameras."

He follows my eyes and sees the small, barely visible eye in the ceiling. When he lowers his gaze back to me, I know I only have seconds. I crouch, preparing for the onslaught.

"You bitch!" he screams, lunging for me. I hear the office door slam and I know Cole's done his part, recording everything, and, hopefully, calling the cops. I also know the office is on the other side of the pool and he won't get to me in time.

Crouching further, I lower my shoulder,

managing to take Cody by surprise for only a moment. He bounces off me once, but lunges again before I can get reset. Grabbing me by the hair, he tosses me to the ground, crawling on top of me. I thrash and buck, freeing myself long enough to scramble to my feet and see Cole grappling with Justin. I take one step and I'm hit from the side, Cody and me both barreling into the pool.

EIGHTEEN

THE WATER ISN'T WARM, BUT IT'S NOT EXACTLY cold either. It's the temperature of a bathtub you've been sitting in for too long. For a moment, I'm too disoriented to do anything but hold my breath. Then dread sets in and I kick for the surface, breaking it for only a second before a pair of hands pushes me back under. I open my eyes, but everything is blurred, bubbles and distortion.

Adrenaline flooding my veins like fire, I thrash and kick wildly, trying to pry his hands off me. It's my nightmare all over again. My lungs burn, convulsing with the need to draw breath. I struggle, but I can feel my body growing heavy and I'm sinking, deeper into the bright blue water. The last of my breath escapes in a rush of bubbles, rising to the surface without me. There's a sound in my ears. It sounds like the crashing of the ocean, far away and close at the same time.

Don't let go, a voice whispers.

I want to cry because the voice is smooth and

familiar. It's my mother's voice.

Don't let go.

My body shudders, convulsing as it fights to find oxygen. The hands release me, but I can't find the strength to push to the surface. My legs are stone, pulling me toward the bottom of the pool. Finally unable to hold it back any longer, I take a breath and water fills my lungs. It's a pain like nothing I've ever experienced. Even as my body rebels against the foreign substance, I slip further and further away.

Don't let go.

In the dim, fading light, I see Cole's face above me. I don't even know if it's real or just the last, desperate wishes of my mind. I'm not sure how I find the strength, but I manage to reach up, stretching my hand upward in the water.

Another hand clasps it, flesh on flesh, pulling me up through the water like plucking a flower. As soon as my head breaks the surface, I sputter, retching the last of the water from my body, gasping, clinging to Cole, who slowly drags us both toward the side of the pool.

When we reach the edge, I take hold, wiping my face. "See," I manage hoarsely. "I told you it would work."

He rolls his eyes and splashes me.

WE'RE BARELY OUT OF THE WATER WHEN THE POLICE

arrive. Justin lays on the floor, knocked out cold but otherwise fine. Cody is gone, probably fleeing as soon as he heard the sirens. I flop onto my back, catching my breath while Cole begins explaining what happened. The EMTs arrive and check us both over, something I'm getting way too familiar with. One more physical and I'm going to have to send Christmas cards.

We have to answer a lot of questions back at the police station. The cops catch up with Cody a few miles from the school and bring him in. I watch as they half drag him through the station, as he screams and cries. There's not much he can do except lawyer up and shut up, but even that won't save him. They ask me to press charges, but I decline. It's just more paperwork and they have it all on tape anyway. They don't really need me. He confessed to murder, after all. He's not going anywhere for a good long time, I don't care what kind of money his family has.

From my seat in the waiting area, I watch them lead Justin, handcuffed, down the hall. His eyes meet mine for only a minute before he looks away. His expression is one of shame, and guilt, and I know he's going to sing like a canary. Maybe they will go easy on him. I have no doubt it was Cody who actually killed Mac. Justin is really just guilty of poor judgment and loving an asshole.

And who hasn't been there?

Finally done with his own interview, Cole flops

into the chair beside me, shaking the last of the water from his hair. "We've got to stop meeting this way, Farris. Wet, cold, and in the police station."

He drapes an arm around me, kissing the side of my head when I lean my head on his shoulder. Laughing resignedly, he says, "We're going to have to start scoring our dates based on body count and blood loss."

"You know the worst part of all of this?" I ask.

"That it all could have been avoided if Cody had been brave enough to step up and admit who he really was instead of hiding? Or that you almost drowned right in front of me? Because I'm still pretty shaken up about the latter."

I frown. "I was actually just thinking about my tablet. That thing cost a fortune. I'm considering making Cho buy me a new one. She owes me, big time."

I feel him chuckle. "That's my girl. Always doing the dumb thing."

The same officer from our first visit took my statement this time, her mouth drawn in a tight, narrow line. Detective Walters. That's her name. Now she walks over, in her sensible flats and tweed blazer, her ginger hair bouncing with each step. "You two are free to go," Walters says reluctantly. "But in the future, I'd caution you to leave the police work to the actual police."

Narrowing my eyes, I open my mouth to say

something about them doing their jobs right in the first place, but Cole covers my mouth with his hand.

Clever boy.

"Yes, Officer. Thank you. As always, you are a paragon of kindness, and that jacket is quite flattering as well."

She glares, pointing toward the exit.

We turn, collect our belongings, and walk out of the station. Once we're out in the chilly night air, I feel the first real bites of coldness prickle my skin. As if reading my mind, Cole rubs my arms. They'd brought us in a squad car, so his SUV is still at the school, leaving us with few options.

"Do we call a cab? Walk? Hitch a ride with some shady strangers?" he asks. "Steal a cop car?"

I make a pfft noise. "Rookie. I've already called in the cavalry." Across the street, Kayla honks, flashing her headlights.

"I really do love you," he says, turning to face me. "Just don't, I mean, let's keep this near-death thing to a minimum from now on, okay?"

I chew my bottom lip. "Deal."

Hand in hand, we cross the street and hop in the back of her car.

"You two have fun?" Kayla asks, pulling away from the curb. She's in her panda jammies and her hair is pulled back in a tight braid, her usual bedtime look. Given the hour, she probably had to sneak out to pick us up. That's real friendship. Sneaking out of the house in your pajamas to pick your friend up from the police station, no questions asked.

"It's done. By tomorrow, everyone will know that Mac didn't kill himself. They'll know what really happened," I say flatly. "That's all that matters."

Kayla's eyes connect with mine in the rearview mirror. She mouths, *Thank you* and I offer her a gentle nod.

KAYLA DROPS US BACK AT MY HOUSE AND WE HALF drag ourselves inside, both bone tired. I debate letting it go, just curling up with him and falling asleep. *There will be other nights*, I tell myself. But then I remember—that might not be true. It certainly wasn't true for Mac.

There are a million things waiting out there for us. Things that want to change us, challenge us, bind us, or separate us. A million bugs in the code, just waiting to be triggered.

I quickly make my decision. As soon as he closes the door, locking it behind him, I push him against the wall and kiss him ferociously, like my life depends on it.

He's hesitant at first, then the urgency spreads and he pulls his shirt over his head, his hands sliding up my back, into my hair, then down my arms, grabbing the hem of my lace top. I feel the tips of his fingers on my bare skin and moan. He's so warm, so solid against me. He slowly lifts my shirt over my head and we dance our way to my bedroom, shedding clothes as we go. There's no fear, no questioning. I want him, and I know he wants me. Everything feels *right*. I've been waiting for this feeling for a very long time, and now that I finally found it, I don't plan to waste a moment. If this week has taught me anything, it's that you never know where tomorrow will lead. We have to seize joy when and where we can find it.

I'm going to carpe the shit out of this diem.

Once we hit my room, I slither out of the rest of my clothes, standing nervously in front of him as my heart hammers in my chest, every square inch of my body ready to ignite. I watch as he does the same, letting my eyes wander across his body, trying to remember how to breathe as I take in every curve of him. Behind my back, I tug open my top dresser drawer, my fingers fumbling for one of the foil wrappers I'd tossed in there after school yesterday.

I hold it up and he grins, flipping out the light.

NINETEEN

"I REALIZE THE HONEYMOON IS PROBABLY OVER, BUT do you think that just excuses you from coffee duty?" I ask, tossing my bag over my shoulder as I head down the hallway. "Because it does not." We ditched yesterday, figuring that we earned it after the previous night's events, but I really have to get back today. The overachiever inside me won't allow another day of stacked-up assignments and missed lectures. Besides, people will think we ran off together or something. I grin, because it's not far from the truth.

Catching a glimpse of Cole in the living room, I veer right. He's standing, remote in hand, in front of the TV while the reporter on screen speaks.

"This latest disaster comes on the heels of last month's suicide bombing of..." Her high, nasal voice fades out as I stare at the screen. Flames, wreckage, and overturned trucks on a desert road.

"Where is this?" I ask, watching the grainy images play, a chill creeping up my back.

He doesn't look at me for a second. When he finally glances over his shoulder, his face is pale. "Adana. Outside the base."

My mouth goes dry. Adana. Turkey. Where my dad is scheduled to be leaving in the next few days.

Unless they get to come home early, a voice whispers in my head.

"How old is the footage?" I ask, staring at the grainy images playing on a loop.

He lowers his head, calculating. "They are saying it happened sometime around eleven am local time. So, what's that like... four am here? So four hours old. Give or take."

Dropping my bag, I spin on my heel, heading for my office. I'm already at my computer when Cole walks in.

"What are you going to do?" he asks, leaning against the doorway. His expression is nervous, and rightfully so. I'm never quite as dangerous as I am when I'm behind a computer screen.

I glance up only briefly, my fingers flying across the keyboard. "I'm borrowing a satellite."

"You're what?" He strides into the room. "No, I cannot have heard you correctly."

Finally at the portal, I pause, taking a minute to tuck my hair behind my ears and crack my knuckles before I begin. "I'm going to access the live feed from a Turkish media satellite. I want to see what's going on in real time," I answer, diving into the first layer of security, careful to cover my tracks.

"That is..." Cole hesitates, taking up a position behind me. "A really bad idea and you know it."

The shell opens and I access the mainframe, peeling back layers of security one at a time. Security systems are like onions. You have to peel back all the layers to get to the core. It's tricky and dangerous and worst of all, slow. The dread grows inside me with each click of the keys. I can't stop, can't do anything other than this. If I do, the dread will build up and I'll explode with it. It's the only way to stay sane.

"What can I do?" he finally asks.

"This is going to take a while. Can you make coffee?" I ask, not looking at him. "And maybe call your mom's boyfriend. See if he knows anything we don't."

The hours tick by, my eyes bleary from staring at the screen. Finally, the last layer cracks and I have access to the internal system. Opening the live feed, I see why all they are showing on the news is a three-minute clip on a loop. The convoy, six trucks in all, along with two hummers, is in shambles. Twisted metal, fiery wreckage. Workers are on site, removing bodies, while armed guards stand by, sweeping the area for possible threats. A row of gurneys sits off to the side, each covered with a white sheet. So many. Too many. Thirty-three, by my count. The video is too pixilated to get much detail, but even so, I manage to make out a single arm, detached from its body, laying on the sandy ground.

As I watch, my mouth waters, bile rising up my throat. I barely make it to the trash can in the corner before I throw up. Cole, who has been making phone calls from the other room, runs in, kneeling beside me and holding my hair while I heave up coffee and the three bites of toast he forced on me. Even when it's all gone, I can't stop shaking, can't stop the pain rolling in my stomach.

He says nothing. What can he say? There's nothing that makes this better. No words that are capable of driving away the fear.

Even if Dad's all right, he can't call. Not now. The rational side of my brain knows that. They will be on lockdown. No communication. That's the rule. But soon. Soon, he will.

He'll call as soon as he can. He always calls. He always comes home. I repeat it over and over to myself, trying to force myself to believe it.

I try to find some scrap of comfort, but there's nothing to grasp onto. Finding Cole's arm, I cling to him, desperately, my fingers digging into his flesh. The world is splintering around me, and he's the only solid thing left in the entire universe. If I let go...

Cole opens his mouth to say something, but he's cut off by the ringing of my doorbell.

The sound is like the clamor of a church bell, and the air thickens around me, time slowing to a crawl. I exhale, climbing to my feet. It's like being in a dream. Each step is slow, labored, like walking in quicksand. Nothing feels real.

Beat...

Twenty-four steps to the door.

I feel Cole at my back, waiting, holding his breath even as I hold mine.

Hand on the cold, chrome knob.

Beat...

When I open it, two Marines, both clad in their dress blues, stand waiting.

Twelve brass buttons on black fabric. Blood-red trim. Shiny, polished shoes. I can't bring myself to look at their faces. One of them says my name, introduces himself. I nod, still not breathing. Reaching out, he hands me a small, perfectly folded letter.

I know what's inside. My pulse echoes in my ears.

Beat...

He speaks again, but I've gone deaf, the only noise is the sound of my own heart. My hand trembles, the paper nearly slipping from my grasp.

I try to swallow, and it sticks in my throat.

Beat...

Unfolding the letter, I scan the page.

From the Department of the Navy

Dear Ms. Barnett,

We are sorry to inform you that your father,

Lieutenant Colonel David Winston Barnett, died today in the line of duty...

There's more, but I can't read it. Everything blurs as I begin to fall.

Beat...

My heart pounds against my ribs like a sledgehammer. Each hit threatening to shatter me like glass.

Beat...

I feel hands reach out, but it doesn't matter. They can't catch me. Can't help me. Can't save me.

Beat...

I'm collapsing inside, folding in on myself, a dying star becoming a black hole. Everything is pain and burning and emptiness. This is death. This is what it feels like to die.

Beat...

I gasp, breathing in but unable to breathe out. I'm drowning again, only this time, there is no surface to swim to, no hand to hold.

Beat...

Darkness falls, and I fall inside of it. A void. Nothing left now. It's almost over.

Beat...

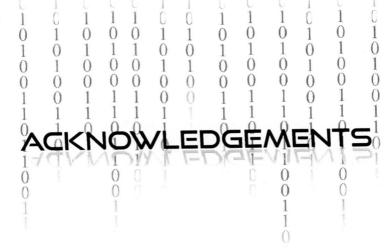

ACKNOWLEDGEMENTS

THERE ARE MANY PEOPLE WHO GO INTO THE creation of a book, and I want to take a moment to give credit where credit is due. I'm very lucky to have an amazing team in Clean Teen Publishing. Marya, Courtney, Beckie, Cynthia, and Mel. Thank you so much for all you do. I know I can be a lot to handle sometimes but you always make me feel like family. I've seen you turn my roughest drafts into beautiful polished novels, and it means more to me than you know.

I'm immeasurably grateful to all the bloggers and reviewers who help me spread the word about my books. Every time you share a cover or leave a review, I feel like the luckiest girl in the world, because you are helping make my dreams come true and I could not do it without you. This goes double for my Street Squad. You guys are awesome!

Of course I would be remiss not to thank my incredible husband Jeremy who has the patience of a saint and the strength of a steel pillar. He's my rock, my partner, and my best friend and he deserves much more praise than I give him. Love you babe.

And last but never least, thanks to all my friends and fans who share their love and support with me every day. Thanks for going on this incredible journey with me and for keeping my head in the clouds and my feet on the ground.

~XOXP

ABOUT THE AUTHOR

SHERRY D. FICKLIN IS A FULL TIME WRITER FROM Colorado where she lives with her husband, four kids, two dogs, and a fluctuating number of chickens and house guests. A former military brat, she loves to travel and meet new people. She can often be found browsing her local bookstore with a large white hot chocolate in one hand and a towering stack of books in the other. That is, unless she's on deadline at which time she, like the Loch Ness monster, is only seen in blurry photographs.

31901059549149

9 781634 221634